J
Faralla, Dana   Feb. 1966
Wonderful flying-go-round.

THE WONDERFUL FLYING-GO-ROUND

The Wonderful Flying-Go-Round

DANA FARALLA

Illustrated by Harold Berson

THE WORLD
PUBLISHING COMPANY
Cleveland and New York

For Jean Tennant

Published by The World Publishing Company
2231 West 110th Street, Cleveland 2, Ohio
Published simultaneously in Canada by
Nelson, Foster & Scott Ltd.
Library of Congress Catalog Card Number: 65-19721 √
FIRST EDITION
WP
Text copyright © 1965 by Dana Faralla
Illustrations copyright © 1965 by The World Publishing Company
Designed by Jack Jaget.

J

Contents

The Amazing Arrival
of the Florabellas

One day a very strange thing happened, so strange that Michael and Randy were to remember it always and talk of it for years to come: *The Amazing Arrival of the Florabellas.*

It happened on the day they launched the red kite.

It was a very special kite, fashioned of thin laths of wood and red paper with a pattern of gold and silver stars. On it there was written a secret word, *Mira-Rami*—"MI" for Michael, and "RA" for Randy, brother and sister. Michael was ten and Randy was eight, and though Michael had often made kites, this was the largest and finest of them all. They had found the star-spangled paper in the Dump Yard one morning, tossed about in the wind like a homeless bird. The paper had probably once been used as wrapping for a Christmas parcel, and someone, having no further need for it, had thrown it away. That was the fate of almost everything that was broken and old, useless and unwanted. It came to rest in the Dump Yard, a deep hollow outside the town where rubbish was dumped.

The Dump Yard was forbidden ground to most children, but for Michael and Randy it was the only place where they could play. They lived in Shanty Town, which was no town at all, only a few shacks and tumble-down houses of the poor at the edge of the main town. Mr. O'Rafferty, their grandfather, said that this land had once been a meadow where sheep and cattle grazed, and there had been a horse fair and a camp of gypsy caravans. The Dump Yard had been known then as Dingle Dell, a cool, green place of trees and ferns. But the town had grown large, stretching and pushing itself out of its boundaries. Now the meadow was gone, and the trees and the gypsy wagons. All around Shanty Town there were factories with chimney stacks pouring out clouds of black smoke. Even the name Dingle Dell had been forgotten by everyone but Mr. O'Rafferty. He spoke of it sometimes as though it were a place he had dreamed about.

Michael and Randy never spoke of it as the "Dump Yard." To them it was a special country with a secret name, a place of surprises, a treasure-trove. They did not see it as a rubbish heap but as a country of hills and mountains and valleys set in a great Pudding Basin scooped out of the flat ground. It was a country with a changing landscape, depending on what had been dumped there or removed. That was part of its charm. On no two days was it quite the same. Valleys disappeared, mountains rose or fell; hills, in turn, became mountains. The most enduring was the Iron Mountain, made largely of old cookstoves, bedsteads, boilers, and lengths of rusting pipe through which rain water sometimes ran in rivulets.

Surrounding the valleys were hills and mountains made of tin cans and old kitchen pots and pans that gleamed like polished silver one day and turned rusty brown the next. On the summits and in the crevasses there were patches like snow, though this was really broken china and crockery. It was a country of glaciers too, and crystal caves of jelly glasses, mustard pots, pickle jars, and window glass that flashed like prisms in the sun. Here, and on the high and perilous cliffs of bricks and flagstones, the children found bits of colored glass, red, green, blue, and yellow. Randy was nearly certain they were rare gems: rubies, emeralds, sapphires, and topaz. She had filled a square biscuit tin with them and had hidden it in the oven of an old cookstove in the Iron Mountain— or, to be more exact, a mountain cave.

Like most countries it was green in the spring and early summer, a jungle of vines and weeds and field flowers from the lost meadow. Never was there a garden more wild and untamed. The wind had sown the seeds. Woodbine, ivy, and morning-glory trailed over everything, using old bedsprings and wire fencing as trellises and arbors. Garlands fell from the cliffs like green waterfalls, or climbed the hills and mountains. Weeds and wild flowers grew along the rim of the Pudding Basin and sprouted out of cracks and fissures in the mountains. Here, too, on the rim of the Pudding Basin there was a little grove of elderberry bushes, and in the valley one of the bushes had rooted itself in an empty barrel. A pumpkin, fat and round as a green goblin child, was growing in an old wicker baby carriage. Stray cats, some striped like tigers, others black as panthers, roamed through the jungle, stalking the mice who lived in the cliffs or in the mountain caves.

Michael and Randy went each day to the Dump Yard, bent on some new discovery to surprise themselves and their grandfather. Mr. O'Rafferty collected rags and tatters and sold them for a few pennies. These would be made into paper. He collected books and papers too, and sold them by weight. These also would be remade into paper again. Whatever the children found they carried back to the little house in Shanty Town in a cart that had lost one of its wheels. Mr. O'Rafferty would put on his spectacles and look over everything slowly and carefully to see if it might be put to any use. When he saw the wonderful red paper spangled with gold and silver stars, he agreed at once that it was meant for a kite.

"A kite made of this paper will take to the wind like the sail of a ship," said Mr. O'Rafferty, who had once been a sailor.

"Or like a bird," said Michael.

"One and the same thing," said Mr. O'Rafferty. "They are all children of the wind."

It was true. The kite, when finished and rising in flight, looked like the sail of a boat in a blue sea of sky, and like the wing of a great red bird. The Mira-Rami kite was indeed a child of the wind. It soared upward from the top of the Iron Mountain, its long tail adorned with bits of colored ribbon like small wings and butterflies, the gold and silver stars on the red paper flashing in the sun.

Michael held the end of the long string attached to the frame of the kite and ran in a circle around the rim of the Pudding Basin, while the wonderful red kite traced another circle in the sky. He held the string loosely to give the kite its freedom in the wind. Randy ran with him, her dark hair like a blackbird's wing, and her tattered dress billowing like a little sail. She was pretending to be both bird and kite herself. Faster and faster the children ran with the red kite high above them. The kite seemed happy in the sky, eager for release, pulling and tugging at the string. Michael, holding the string more tightly now, felt it grow taut. It was he who was pulling and tugging, trying to curb the flight.

"The string isn't long enough," he said in dismay. "The kite is climbing too high."

A sudden gust of wind, and the string slipped from his grasp. The red kite flew upward on the currents of air with the swift grace of a bird. It was free, and beautiful it looked, bright red in a blue sky. Higher and higher it climbed, like the skylark that hides itself in the clouds. Soon it was only a speck of red with a little glint of gold where its painted stars reflected the beams of the sun.

For a long time the children stood on the rim of the Pudding Basin, looking upward, shielding their eyes with their hands against the glare of the sun. The kite was gone and the sky seemed lonely without it, and yet it was still there somewhere, though out of sight.

"It was the most wonderful kite I ever made," Michael said with both pride and regret.

"I expect it will come back when the wind stops," Randy said, trying to be cheerful.

It was a disappointment, of course, and yet they could not really be sad on such a bright, sunny day in June. They could even understand a little why the red kite would want to be free. They themselves felt like flying. If there was ever a day meant for flying, it was this. Blue sky, a few fleecy white clouds, and a fresh breeze blowing.

"We'll probably find something wonderful here today," said Randy. She was picking wild flowers, mostly buttercups and small white daisies. "I feel like a surprise."

"The best surprise would be to see the kite again," said Michael.

They climbed from the rim of the Pudding Basin to the Iron Mountain and sat down on a green plateau. It was really the top of the cookstove in which the jewels were hidden, but it was so covered with morning-glory vines that no one could see the secret cave. From here they could view their special country, looking across mountain tops and into the valleys. Never had it looked so green and fresh. They ate the last of their breakfast, two sugared buns. It was a special treat. Mr. O'Rafferty and the baker

11

had made a trade: an old stove poker for a paper bag of buns. A very fair deal, for if anyone had use for a stove poker it was the baker, and if anyone at all had use for a bag of sugared buns it was the O'Raffertys.

A cat the color of bright sunshine leaped out of the jungle, chasing a white butterfly. They laughed to see Taffy pawing the air, trying to fly.

"You'll need wings yourself to catch it," they said.

Taffy the cat was rather wild, but had long ago recognized Michael and Randy as friends. He let the butterfly go on its zigzag journey and begged now for a few tidbits left in the paper bag, purring and rubbing against the children's bare legs. Then suddenly the cat stiffened, alert and listening, its head lifted. Was it the butterfly again, within reach, perched for a moment on a daisy? Was it a bird in an elderberry bush on the rim of the Pudding Basin? The children glanced upward, idly curious. Something, a very small object, was floating slowly downward from the sky. A hawk, perhaps, its wings almost motionless, riding the waves of air.

"What can it be?" the children said, shading their eyes against the sun so that they might see better.

"Probably a bird, flying high," said Michael.

"Maybe it is the kite coming back," said Randy.

"But this looks brown, and the kite is red—"

"I'm sure there is something red floating there, above the bird or whatever it is."

"Yes, yes!" Michael said excitedly. "There *is* something red. It could be both the kite *and* a bird."

"Now it looks more like a nest than a bird. But how could a nest fall out of a tree in the sky?"

"It's a balloon!" Michael shouted in excitement. "It's a red balloon tied to a basket!"

At first hardly larger than a ripe red cherry, the balloon became large as a plum, and then large and round as an apple. It was coming nearer, carrying with it a basket no larger than a thimble, then large as a sparrow's nest, and now as large as a straw hat.

"It's coming nearer! It's going to land!"

The basket was now larger than the largest wash basket, and so near that the children could see the net of ropes attached to its rim, holding captive the balloon. Flags and fringes and bits of colored ribbon were tied to the ropes, fluttering in the breeze quite like the tail of the vanished red kite. Two figures leaned over the side of the basket, one in a brown bowler hat and the other in a wide-brimmed hat of blue velvet with pink ostrich plumes. A little man and a little lady. As the balloon basket came nearer, the children saw that the man was peering down at them through a long tube, a kind of spying-glass, and the little lady was smiling and waving to them with a pink lace handkerchief. Both seemed to be talking in excitement, but nothing could be heard, for the balloon was making a loud wheezing noise like winter wind blowing down a chimney. At the sound, Taffy the cat leaped with fright into the valley and hid in the baby carriage with the green pumpkin child. Already the shadow of the basket was dark upon the Iron Mountain and the rim of the Pudding Basin.

"Watch your head!" shouted Michael. "Here it comes!"

There was a great sighing and wheezing and gasping as the last breath of air was drained from the balloon, and in that moment the basket touched the rim of the Pudding Basin. It thumped and bumped upon the ground, rocking back and forth like a cradle, and then settled itself among the tall weeds. Above it the balloon wafted for a moment like a flag or a red sail waiting for the wind to fill it. Then, with a long, tired sigh, it went completely limp and fell soundlessly upon the tops of the elderberry bushes.

Michael and Randy ran through the weeds along the rim of the Pudding Basin, but already the little man had climbed out of the basket on a rope ladder. He was helping the little lady descend, her long blue velvet skirts lifted daintily above her pink satin slippers.

Never, thought the children, staring in open-mouthed astonishment, had they seen such an amazing couple nor, in truth, such an amazing and unusual arrival.

The Land of Mira-Rami

"Good morning," said the little man pleasantly. He lifted his brown bowler hat. "I am Mr. Florabella, and this is Mrs. Florabella."

"Good morning," said Mrs. Florabella, smiling. "Isn't it a lovely day? We are delighted to be here."

"Good morning," Michael and Randy said rather shyly.

"It is most kind of you to be here to welcome us," said Mr. Florabella.

"We didn't exactly know you were coming," Michael said truthfully.

"Yes, we did," Randy said, finding her voice. "We expected some sort of a surprise today. *I* did, anyway. Have you come from the moon?"

"Goodness no!" said Mrs. Florabella. "Do we look moonstruck?"

Randy did not really know if the Florabellas looked moonstruck. They were certainly a curious pair. They were both very small, not as tall as Randy, nor did they even reach shoulder-high with Michael. They looked rather like children dressed in grown-up clothes. Or were they grownups pretending to be children? It was a little difficult to tell. There was something birdlike about them, too—their nimble grace in climbing down the rope ladder, as though they had not used their feet or hands at all but had flown from the balloon basket. The basket itself was like a bird nest woven out of reeds and dried grass. Mr.

Florabella's dark eyes were certainly bright and quick as a wren's as he regarded the two children, tilting his head from side to side. His black hair, parted in the middle, fell low on his forehead in two shiny wings, and his mustache, with waxed and pointed tips, also had the shape of wings. In the ribbon band of his bowler hat there was a pert little woodcock feather. However, there was nothing birdlike about his coat and trousers, other than the parrot colors—yellow, green, and brown plaid. His shirt was of yellow silk and his cravat of green satin, knotted in a wide butterfly bow. His feet, remarkably small, were shod in black patent-leather and gray spats with pearl buttons. He wore white doeskin gloves —a very proper gentleman. He carried a purple umbrella, the handle resting on his arm like a bracelet of carved ivory. Around his waist there was stretched a gold chain and a large watch that appeared to have no hands. Looking at Mr. Florabella closely, you could not say he was old and you could not say he was young. Having a watch without hands, he had probably lost count of time and days and years.

Mrs. Florabella looked like a painted china doll, so there was no telling her proper age either. Her eyes were the color of blue cornflowers, and her curls, peeping out from under the wide brim of her hat, were as golden as wheat chaff. It was a marvelous hat, trimmed with pink ostrich plumes and ribbon bows. All these little winged bows and waving feathers made her appear birdlike too, even if there had not been a canary sitting there. It was a real bird, not a gold ornament, perched on a pink ostrich plume, chirping and warbling. Mrs. Florabella's dress was also of blue velvet, trimmed with more bows and ribbons, and on her arm she carried a little red velvet coat for chilly days. A feather boa of ostrich plumes like those on the hat was draped over her shoulders, and around her neck there was a heart-shaped gold locket with a red ruby. She, too, wore white doeskin gloves and carried a little handbag of colored beads sewn on crimson silk.

"Come, my pretty," said Mrs. Florabella. She held up a gloved hand, the forefinger curved like a perch for a bird. There was a flutter of wings and the canary alighted on Mrs. Florabella's finger. "This is Carolino," she said smiling. "Carolino always travels with us. We're very fond of music—and of Carolino. Now that you have been introduced, back to your pink feather bush." Mrs. Florabella raised her arm and obediently the canary flew upward to the ostrich plume.

Mrs. Florabella came nearer the children, floating upon the weeds, her little pink satin slippers hidden beneath her long, flowing skirts. "I don't think we quite heard your names." She had a thin, flute-like voice very pleasant to the ears, as though she had taken lessons from her canary.

"We didn't really tell you yet," said Michael. "I'm Michael, and this is Randy my sister."

Randy held out the bouquet of buttercups and daisies, but she was too shy to say anything.

"How perfectly lovely!" said Mrs. Florabella. "How kind of you to pick them for me."

"Michael and Randy," said Mr. Florabella, as though he were savoring the sound of the names.

"Yes," said Mrs. Florabella. "So everything is quite all right, isn't it?"

"Of course! But we were already quite certain before the balloon landed," said Mr. Florabella. He and Mrs. Florabella smiled and nodded at each other, sharing a secret.

"If you didn't come from the moon, then where?" said Randy, who could no longer withhold her curiosity.

"Oh, from here and there," Mrs. Florabella said airily, swinging the beaded bag back and forth. She looked at Mr. Florabella and laughed.

"Is that your country?" said Randy seriously. "Here and there?"

"I suppose so." It was Mr. Florabella who answered. "The whole world is our country. We are great travelers, Mrs. Florabella and I. All we need is an invitation, such as yours."

"Invitation?" said Michael, puzzled.

"We began the descent as soon as we got your message."

"Message?" said Michael, more puzzled than ever. Then he whispered to Randy, "There must be some mistake."

"Though we had only a bird's-eye view of your country," continued Mr. Florabella, "it was quite enough to tell us that we had come to the right place."

"Do you mean the whole country, or just *this?*" Michael said, pointing to the Dump Yard.

"Here, where we have landed," said Mr. Florabella. From his pocket he took out a folded piece of paper that appeared to be a map.

"I don't think you'll find it on any map," said Michael.

"But I don't expect to find it on a map," said Mr. Florabella. "We always go to the undiscovered places, the secret countries. It is we who put them on a map." With a black crayon taken from the handle of his umbrella he drew a circle on the paper, and within the circle an "X" and the number 624. "No special name. Secret land of Michael and Randy. Now for general position." He consulted his watch. The back of it proved to be a compass. Then he marked NORTH, SOUTH, EAST, and WEST on the circle and drew four cherub faces with round, puffed cheeks. They appeared to be blowing wind from their mouths. "Don't worry, my little friends, no one will discover your secret country from this map. I'm only showing which way the wind blows."

"Why?" asked Randy.

"For one thing we travel by balloon. And for another thing— well, that is something we will speak of later. I must discuss it first with Mrs. Florabella. We also have our little secrets."

Where *was* Mrs. Florabella? She had quite disappeared. The children had not noticed this until now, so interested they had been in Mr. Florabella's map.

"Now, if you don't mind I should like to look at your country more closely with my spying-glass," said Mr. Florabella. "Here, from the rim of the canyon—"

"Pudding Basin," Randy said promptly.

"Pudding Basin," said Mr. Florabella. "That's rather jolly. However, I think a country should be named after its discoverers."

"Oh, so do we," said Michael. "The Pudding Basin is only the hole in the ground. The name of the country is secret."

18

"Naturally," said Mr. Florabella, "since it is a secret country." From the rod of the purple umbrella he pulled out a length of bamboo. It was a spying-glass. "*Very* interesting, *very* interesting." He trained the spying-glass upon the hills and mountains in the Pudding Basin. "Remarkably green. Wonderful possibilities! I congratulate you on your discovery."

"I don't know that we exactly discovered it," said Michael. "It's been here for a long time. Everyone in Shanty Town knows about it."

"Yes, but have they ever *discovered* it?" said Mr. Florabella. "There is a difference, you know. People may see a place day in, day out. They *know* it is there. But have they ever *discovered* it, I say again. For instance, they will pass a tree by a roadside every day, but do they ever really see it? Do they know what kind of a tree it is, the shape and pattern of the leaves or the bark, or if there is a bird nest in it? Have they ever touched the tree, felt of the bark to see if it was smooth or rough? Have they ever sat under it or climbed the branches? No. To them it might just as well be a tree painted on a wall or a signboard. The same can be said of your secret country. Have they ever seen the Diamond Glacier or the Crystal Caves? The Iron Mountain and the hills of tin? The jungle and the elderberry forest? No! All they see is a pile of rubbish."

The children looked at each other in astonishment.

"He knows *everything*," whispered Randy.

"People without imagination, people without dreams," said Mr. Florabella. "Not even my spying-glass would help them!" He was about to return the spying-glass to the hollow rod of the umbrella.

"Could I please have a look before you put it away?" said Randy eagerly.

"And I, too?" said Michael.

"It's a very special glass," said Mr. Florabella. "Most people, those without any imagination, never see anything at all through it. And those with imagination don't really need it. And that means *you*."

19

"Then why do *you* look through it?" said Randy.

"You are a very clever little girl," said Mr. Florabella, smiling. "I look through it once a day to be certain I still have an imagination."

"Anyway, I'd like to try," said Randy. She held the bamboo close to one eye. "Oh, lovely green!" she said almost at once. "And a pink tree with a yellow bird in it—"

"That will be Mrs. Florabella walking along the rim of the canyon—the Pudding Basin," said Mr. Florabella. "Point the glass a little lower, my dear."

"Lovely green here too," said Randy. "And something down in the valley going around in a circle—"

"That's quite enough for one day," said Mr. Florabella and he hurriedly took the glass from her.

"But I didn't finish looking," she said. "It was a kind of rainbow whirling."

"You have a greater imagination than I suspected," said Mr. Florabella. He was smiling and looked well pleased.

"Now it's my turn," said Michael determinedly. He, too, held the bamboo rod to his eye. "Everything is wonderful green," he said excitedly. "And a rainbow going in circles."

"So you saw it too," said Mr. Florabella, taking the spying-glass from Michael. "That makes three of us."

"But what was it?" Michael said. "If you'd let me look again—"

"You have seen quite enough," Mr. Florabella said, kindly but

20

firmly. He returned the spying-glass to the rod of the umbrella. "It's a very sensitive instrument, and there is a great amount of sun glare today, especially on the Diamond Glacier."

"Will it hurt your spying-glass?" Randy asked anxiously.

"It might crack the glass and we certainly don't want a cracked view of your secret country, do we? There are already enough people who see it that way. People who dare to call it the Dump Yard."

"Since he seems to know everything, we might as well tell him the secret name," Randy said to Michael in a loud whisper.

"We've never told anyone except Mr. O'Rafferty," said Michael, a little hesitant.

"I appreciate the high honor, but a secret is a secret," said Mr. Florabella, who could not help overhearing them. "Mrs. Florabella and I always share ours. So if you tell me, you must tell her as well."

"No, don't tell me, let me guess!" It was Mrs. Florabella, coming through the weeds and the elderberry bushes. She was smiling and humming a gay little tune in harmony with Carolino. Trailing behind her in single file there were at least a dozen cats, Taffy in the lead—cats of all colors, some striped and some spotted, black, white, gray, orange, yellow. They were staring up at Carolino with lifted heads and adoring eyes, completely fascinated. They had never before seen a canary perched on a pink ostrich plume upon a velvet hat.

"Would it be Mira-Rami?" Mrs. Florabella said. "I do think it is a lovely name, a lovely little country. 'MI' for Michael, and 'RA' for Randy."

"But how did you know?" the children said in surprise.

"Yes, my dear, how ever did you know?" said Mr. Florabella, though it cannot be said that he looked entirely surprised.

"I have a rather good imagination," said Mrs. Florabella. "Besides that, the cats told me. First one and then another, and then all of them together. Like this: *MiiiRaaa-RaaaMiii!* I understood it at once. Listen to them! They're saying it again."

Which in truth they were. First Taffy, and then another, and then all of them together. *MiiiRaaa-RaaaMiii!*

Michael and Randy laughed so hard they nearly fell from the rim of the Pudding Basin into the fabulous Land of Mira-Rami.

Over the Rim

"Now since we have decided to stay we must go to work and get nicely settled," said Mrs. Florabella. She took off her white gloves in a leisurely manner and put them in her little beaded bag.

"Do you intend to stay in Mira-Rami or just on the rim?" Michael asked.

"The rim will do," said Mr. Florabella. "That's where the Sky Bird chose to land. The balloon basket—we not only travel in it but live in it. Like the snail and the tortoise we carry our house with us."

"You mean your *house* carries *you* with it," said Randy.

"That's one way of looking at it," said Mr. Florabella.

The great basket was almost hidden in the tall weeds, the balloon still resting on the top of the elderberry bushes, limp as a wet cloth. They all walked around the Sky Bird, inspecting it— that is nearly around it, for one end of the basket was on the very edge of the Pudding Basin, without enough room even for Taffy to walk there.

"What a darling house!" said Randy. "It must be like living in a bird nest. When we saw it in the sky we thought it *was* a nest."

"Isn't it a bit too near the edge?" said Michael.

"Perhaps," said Mr. Florabella with no concern. "You might move it a little for us. You seem to be a sturdy lad. However, we'll unload it first, which means we must ask the cats to leave. Curiosity once killed a cat."

"Also a cat once swallowed a canary," said Michael.

23

"Oh, Carolino is quite wise to their ways. But Project 624 must remain a secret."

"Project 624?" said the children with interest.

"Yes, of course! We finished Project 623 yesterday, so now we're on Project 624."

"That's simple arithmetic," commented Mrs. Florabella.

"I suppose I must go fishing," said Mr. Florabella cheerfully. "That's the best way of luring cats from secret projects."

"But there aren't any lakes or riv—" Michael said, and stopped abruptly.

Mr. Florabella pretended not to hear. Whistling merrily, he walked along the rim of the Pudding Basin. "In all these mountain streams there must be hundreds of sardines."

He held his umbrella over the land of Mira-Rami, the purple cloth still wound tightly around the rod, the tip pointed downward—a fishing pole without a line. The dusty weeds suddenly appeared to be tall water reeds and marsh grass. Something shining like silver flew through the air—a fish leaping out of water. Stuck to the tip of the umbrella was an empty sardine tin, not yet rusty. Already Taffy and the other cats were beside Mr. Florabella, sniffing and crying out. He removed the tin from the umbrella and tossed it far off among the weeds, while the cats went in swift pursuit.

"There is sure to be a bit of oil left in the tin and a small tail or fin," said Mr. Florabella. "And the lovely odor of sardine almost never vanishes."

"Is your umbrella magnetized or something?" asked Michael, curious.

"Only the tip. My own idea, of course!"

Mr. Florabella would have been content to stay all day in the shade of the elderberry bushes fishing for sardines from the streams of Mira-Rami, but Mrs. Florabella was eager to set their house in order. With his umbrella still hooked on his arm Mr. Florabella went nimbly up the rope ladder of the balloon basket.

The Sky Bird was lined with crimson velvet, padded with eider-down for flying power. All around the inside there was a circular bench of reeds cushioned with more velvet and eider-down.

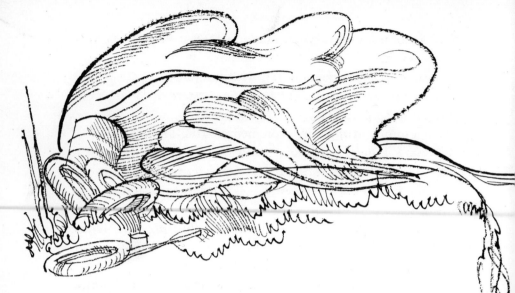

Underneath the bench various bundles and parcels had been stored, which Mr. Florabella now pulled out or poked with the magnetized tip of the umbrella. He began handing them down to Michael and Randy.

First there was a blue teapot, the sight of which delighted Mrs. Florabella.

"A gift from the emperor of China," she said.

"That must have been a long time ago," said Michael, who had learned a thing or two from Mr. O'Rafferty.

"I expect so," agreed Mrs. Florabella. "And there's still not a crack in it."

Next there was a picnic basket holding a little round kettle in which there were tin plates, soup bowls, folding drinking cups— two of each.

"Everything fits together," said Randy in admiration.

"Like a Chinese puzzle," said Mrs. Florabella. "That's another idea we got in China."

"You seem to have been *everywhere.*"

"Here and there, mostly. There's still time for *everywhere.*"

Down came a bundle of bamboo sticks tied with tasseled cord, a roll of blue sailcloth, and a canvas satchel with a heart-shaped lock. Then two folding campstools with red velvet seats, and two

26

cushions and a coverlet, also of red velvet. That was all. Oh, yes, there was also a little gilded bird cage.

"I guess you like red velvet," said Randy.

"It's royal velvet," said Mrs. Florabella proudly and she sat down on one of the cushions. She was holding the blue teapot and the bouquet of flowers, which was beginning to wilt. "It came from the Royal Box, you know, where the king and queen sit at the opera. Paris or London, I don't quite remember where."

"A box?" said Randy, puzzled. "The king and queen sit in a box?"

"Yes, on golden chairs set inside a box, all done up in red velvet."

"How can they see if they're in a box?"

"My dear, it's the best possible position. The box is fastened to the wall, near the stage. All you need to do is lean over the edge, just as we do from the balloon basket."

"How did you get the velvet out of the Royal Box?" Randy persisted.

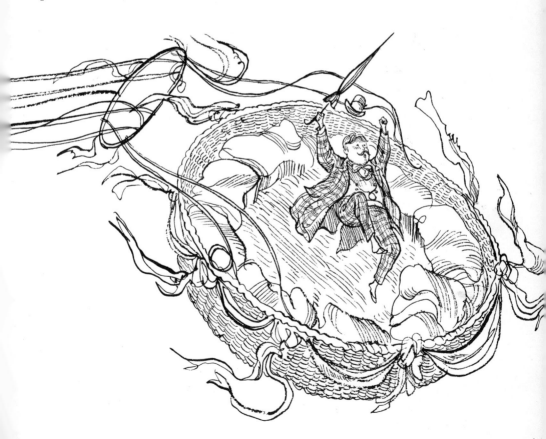

"Mr. Florabella must have bargained for it," said Mrs. Florabella vaguely and she yawned. "The mice and moths had nibbled it nearly to tatters. The box had to be relined. We cut out all the holes, and the velvet is quite as good as new."

"You cut out all the holes?"

"Yes, with scissors. Then we filled them up again. I sewed patches on them, *square* patches, which are much easier than round ones if you know anything about sewing. Which reminds me, Mr. Florabella has forgotten my sewing basket."

"But, my dear, do you need it now?" said Mr. Florabella. He was halfway down the rope ladder, mopping his brow with a little red-and-white checkered tablecloth.

"You know I always put the biscuits and the tea-caddy in it, and it's nearly teatime."

"Teatime!" said Randy. "We've hardly finished breakfast."

"That's the fun of having a watch without hands," said Mrs. Florabella. "You can have tea whenever you like."

"Wherever did you put the sewing basket?" Mr. Florabella called. "Ah, here it is! You hung it on a hook where the balloon rope should be fastened."

There was a brief glimpse of Mr. Florabella at the far end of the Sky Bird, leaning over the rim and holding the sewing basket triumphantly aloft. Michael, Randy, and Mrs. Florabella watched in speechless horror, for in that same moment the Sky Bird tilted over the edge of the Pudding Basin. Mr. Florabella jumped from the circular bench to the other side of the Sky Bird to restore balance. But it was too late. The balloon basket teetered and swayed, and then fell with a thundering crash into the Land of Mira-Rami, carrying with it Mr. Florabella.

Happy Landing!

The Sky Bird in its downward plunge struck the summit of a mountain, snow-capped with kitchen crockery. First a soup tureen went flying through the air, and then broken cups and saucers, plates and platters, pickle jars and jelly glasses. An avalanche thundered down into the valley—tin cans, pots and pans, tiles, bricks, plaster, iron pipes, and bedsprings—not to mention the cats of Mira-Rami, who went leaping and flying out of the country, frightened out of their wits. The balloon basket and the Land of Mira-Rami were completely hidden in a gray, smoking cloud of dust.

"Mr. Florabella! Mr. Florabella! Where are you?"

There was no answer, only the rumble of falling bricks and stones, the rattle of tin cans, the crash of broken glass and dishes.

"Mr. Florabella! Mr. Florabella!"

The dust was beginning to lift, and slowly the country reappeared, viewed as if through a curtain. The Sky Bird could be dimly seen now, floating upon gray clouds, or so it seemed. However, it was set firmly enough on the top of the cookstove, the vine-covered plateau of the Iron Mountain. The stove was the only landmark that remained the same. Everything else was changed and altered. Mr. Florabella rose unsteadily from the bottom of the basket and leaned over the side facing the rim of the Pudding Basin where Mrs. Florabella, Michael, and Randy stood anxiously looking down and calling to him. He could not see them, nor anything at all, for the bowler hat had slipped down over his eyes, the brim touching his nose. He was covered with dust, quite as though he had fallen into a barrel of ashes. His winged mustache was entirely white.

"Will somebody take this sewing basket out of my hands so I can take off my hat and see what is going on!" he said, coughing and sneezing.

"Just set it down anywhere," said Mrs. Florabella.

Mr. Florabella obliged her by dropping the sewing basket over the side of the Sky Bird.

Mrs. Florabella uttered a shrill, flute-like scream. "Oh, the biscuits! They'll be broken into bits!"

Mr. Florabella took off his hat. He looked very comical, completely powdered with dust except for the top of his head, his shiny black hair looking like a round skullcap. He undid his green satin cravat and began using it as a duster. Mrs. Florabella was about to throw him her feather boa but thought better of it, and tossed him the red-and-white checkered tablecloth instead. It fell far short of the mark, landing in the rubble.

"Oh, a pity! It was so useful as a chessboard!"

"As soon as the dust settles we'll come down and pull the basket up with the balloon ropes," said Michael. "But you'll have to get out first. The basket will be too heavy with you in it. Can you see to climb down the ladder now?"

"Of course I can see," said Mr. Florabella, rubbing dust out of his eyes. "However, I intend to remain with the Sky Bird just as any captain would aboard his ship in disaster—land or sea or sky."

"But we can't pull you up, Sky Bird and all," Michael said rather desperately.

"He'll manage well enough," said Mrs. Florabella confidently. "That is, if he's still got the umbrella."

Mr. Florabella leaned over the rim of the basket, pulling the net of ropes and the limp balloon toward him as though he had caught a great red fish in a sea of gray dust.

"Where is the umbrella?" shouted Mrs. Florabella.

"On my arm, of course!"

30

"Oh, so it is! It's turned quite gray. I didn't recognize it at first."

Mr. Florabella had now removed the magnetized tip and had opened the umbrella halfway so that it took the shape of a bellows. This was another of his amazing ideas. The bellows began blowing into the balloon, and before long little bumps and mounds appeared in the red silk.

"Does he use gas or air?" asked Michael in puzzlement.

"Air," said Mrs. Florabella promptly. "There's so much of it around, so why not use it?" She smiled encouragingly at the children. "He doesn't need to blow the balloon to full size. With all the luggage gone, the basket is light as a feather."

The balloon was rising within the net of ropes, beginning to take the shape of a globe. Soon it was floating above the basket and the Sky Bird rocked back and forth trying to rise from the plateau.

"I can't get it started," Mr. Florabella shouted, and then disappeared at the bottom of the basket. "The pull of the Iron Mountain is too strong."

"Point the umbrella the other way," shouted Michael. "Point it upward, away from the stove—the plateau, I mean."

"The magnetized tip is in my pocket! I can't get at it."

"Stand on your head!" shouted Mrs. Florabella. "Maybe it will fall out of your pocket."

"I *am* standing on my head!"

Suddenly the basket lifted itself from the cookstove plateau, and then with a thud it abruptly settled down again. Then up, then down, as though trying to pull itself free of sticky fly-paper or glue. Each time it struck the plateau, whiffs of smoke poured out of the basket—the dust in the eider-down and velvet, filtering out through the woven reeds. Then surprisingly the basket leaped upward as though a fire had been started in the cookstove, too hot for comfort.

"I'm off!" shouted Mr. Florabella, the tip of the umbrella now pointed skyward and showing high above the rim of the basket.

The Sky Bird flew upward and began circling the rim of the

Pudding Basin. Michael and Randy and Mrs. Florabella followed the flight, running through the dusty weeds and bushes as if they were chasing each other in a comical game of tag. Mr. Florabella was no longer standing on his head but had climbed up on the reed bench and was looking down, making signs and motions. Already the balloon was shrinking, making whistling and sighing sounds. The bottom of the basket brushed the tops of the tallest elderberry bushes.

"Grab the mooring ropes," shouted Mr. Florabella.

Down came the basket and set itself with a great sound of sighing upon a clump of weeds in the shadow of the elderberry grove, a safe three steps away from the rim of the Pudding Basin.

"Happy landing!"

Jauntily Mr. Florabella climbed down the rope ladder, none the worse for his adventure, except for a thin film of dust remaining on his clothing and the tips of his mustache. The umbrella, half open in the shape of a bellows, still hung on his arm.

"I could certainly do with a nice cup of tea!" said Mr. Florabella.

Tea and Crumb Cakes

Tea was a little slow in the making. First, the tea-caddy and the biscuits were in the sewing basket somewhere in the Land of Mira-Rami. Second, there was no stove. Also there was no water.

Mr. Florabella sat on a campstool, making out a list of what was needed. He had a pack of small white cards in his pocket on which he wrote everything, one card for each article.

"It's easier this way," he said. "Instead of crossing out something on a list, you just throw a card away—though sometimes we keep them if it happens to be teatime. Mrs. Florabella uses them to start the fire under the kettle."

This was the list:

> 6 wooden stakes (a good half dozen)
> Hammer for pounding stakes
> Stones or bricks to make stove (prefer bricks)
> Iron cooking grill
> Fresh water
> Vase for Mrs. F's bouquet
> 2 extra cups
> 2 extra plates or saucers
> Firewood (dry)

He shuffled the cards and then asked Michael and Randy to draw one from the pack, until they each had four cards. One remained. "I'll add another," said Mr. Florabella. *"Pail for carry-*

ing water. No doubt you'll find everything in the Land of Mira-Rami."

"Aren't you going with us?" Michael said, a little surprised.

"No," said Mr. Florabella lazily. "You know the country better than I. Besides, I've already had a rather strenuous day."

"Are you going with us, Mrs. Florabella?" Randy asked.

"No, my dear. I never climb mountains in these slippers," Mrs. Florabella said and she lifted her skirts a wee bit to show her pink satin slippers. "Nor does Mr. Florabella in his lovely black patent-leather shoes, especially now with all the dust."

It was merely an excuse. The Florabellas did not fancy work unless it seemed like play.

"Which things do you want first?" asked Michael.

"First things first," said Mr. Florabella. "Bricks for the stove, iron grill, firewood."

"Water," said Mrs. Florabella, sitting down on the other camp-stool. "Water for the tea, and a little extra for Carolino. He likes a bath sometimes in the kettle, don't you, my pet?"

Carolino, hopping about on the rim of the velvet hat, chirped a ready answer.

"And you, too, I suppose," Randy said pleasantly.

Mrs. Florabella did not reply. She was using her feather boa as a duster, flicking off the dust from Mr. Florabella's patent-leather shoes.

"It may take a little time to find everything because of the avalanche," Michael said. "And the nearest pump is in Shanty Town."

"Time?" said Mr. Florabella, looking at his watch without hands. "We have all the time in the world. . . ."

Michael and Randy returned from the mountains and valleys of Mira-Rami more in need of a bath than Carolino. Mrs. Florabella said a good dusting-off with her feather boa would be quite enough. She and Mr. Florabella set the children to work at once building the outdoor stove, showing them how to arrange the bricks and stones, leaving an opening at the bottom for a draft of air. The Florabellas were very clever about explaining things and giving orders without doing much work themselves.

"Will this chicken wire do?" said Michael. "We couldn't find an iron grill."

"I like it better," said Mrs. Florabella with delight. "It's as dainty as a spider's web." At once she put the kettle on to boil. "Water! You've forgotten the fresh water."

"We haven't forgotten it," said Randy. "We just haven't had time. Besides, we couldn't find a pail. We'll have to use pickle jars and bottles instead."

"All the time in the world," said Mrs. Florabella gaily. It was one of their favorite expressions.

And so, with all the time in the world, Michael and Randy were slow in fetching the water. There is no pleasanter thing in summer than running water, unless it be a shady tree. They stood under the pump in Shanty Town and washed the dust of Mira-Rami from their hands and faces, their heads and feet, and got thoroughly splashed and wet. Mr. O'Rafferty was at the pump too, floating paper boats in a washtub that leaked. He was much too busy pumping water into the washtub to ask any questions. It seemed entirely natural to him that Michael and Randy should

be rinsing out old bottles and pickle jars. When crystal-clear, the children filled them with water, now cold as a mountain stream.

"Lovely for lemonade, but much too cold for tea," said Mrs. Florabella when they returned. "And where *is* the tea?"

"In the tea-caddy in your sewing basket—where you always keep it," said Mr. Florabella, yawning.

"I'm sure Michael and Randy will fetch it," said Mrs. Florabella. She was arranging the wilted bouquet in the smallest pickle jar. "They have been so clever about everything else."

"Couldn't Mr. Florabella just use the tip of his umbrella and fish for it?" said Randy, for she was tired. "Especially if there are needles and pins in the basket."

"I'll fish for it," said Michael.

Since this was more play than work, Mr. Florabella aroused himself, and presently the sewing basket, looking very dusty, was dangling from the tip of the umbrella.

"Oh, our biscuits!" Mrs. Florabella exclaimed, lifting the cover from the basket. There wasn't one to be seen, only broken bits and crumbs. "Never mind, we'll make crumb cakes instead. They taste quite the same as biscuits. Randy shall help me."

"I don't think I know how to make crumb cakes," said Randy.

"It's quite easy if you've ever made sand cakes or mud pies, and I'm sure you have. Here is the recipe if you'd like to write it down on one of the cards."

"I think I'd rather taste them first," said Randy.

"Fill two folding drinking cups with biscuit crumbs," said Mrs. Florabella. "Sprinkle with cold water until nicely sticky. Press firmly together with your thumb. Place in the sun to dry. Turn cups upside down on a saucer. Serve and eat. Could anything be simpler? For four people you use four folding cups. In season, I sometimes use wild-strawberry or blackberry juice instead of water. It makes a nice change."

While the crumb cakes were sun-baking, Mrs. Florabella told Randy to lay the red-and-white checkered tablecloth upon the weeds, and the dishes as well.

"But the cloth is down in Mira-Rami where you threw it, don't you remember?" said Randy. And then mischievously she added, "Carolino can fetch it in his beak."

But Carolino was in no mood for errands. The canary was pecking at stray biscuit crumbs hidden among the yarns and embroidery threads in the sewing basket.

"I have just the thing for a picnic cloth," said Mr. Florabella, who had a ready answer for every problem. He unlocked the canvas satchel and took out a folded sheet of paper which he spread upon the ground. "Project 624! What could be more fitting for our first tea party in Mira-Rami?"

Here it was again, that mysterious number!

"Six two four?" said the two children, frowning a little.

"Yes, Project 624," repeated Mr. Florabella. "It was mentioned earlier in the day, and here it is before your eyes, the reason for our coming here." He pointed his umbrella to a circle drawn on the paper rather like the one on the map he had made of Mira-

Rami, though this circle had twelve numbers within it: a clock face without hands.

"We still don't understand."

"But it's very simple," said Mr. Florabella. "Whatever way you add the numbers, six, two, and four, you are certain to get twelve. Try it and see. Backwards or forwards it always comes out the same. Twelve."

In a kind of bewilderment Michael and Randy began counting on their fingers.

"Tea is ready!" called Mrs. Florabella gaily. "Tea and crumb cakes!"

The Painted Wigwam

"What exactly is Project 624?" said Michael. "Even if it does add up to twelve—" He and Randy had been trying to ask this all during teatime, but Mrs. Florabella always changed the subject.

"More tea?" said Mrs. Florabella brightly. The blue teapot was now quite empty, but she continued pouring it just the same. Michael and Randy were drinking out of Mira-Rami jelly glasses, for the Florabellas had only two folding cups. "I do think tea looks lovely in glasses. Like melted taffy. In fact I sometimes make it out of taffy and hot water. Did you know that Russians always drink tea out of glasses?"

"No," said Randy. "We didn't know."

"We learned that from a Russian himself," said Mrs. Florabella. "A bear trainer in our company. He had a brown dancing bear named Pushkin, so named I suppose because it always had to be pushed a little before it would start dancing." She daintily picked a crumb out of a crumb cake and fed it to Carolino. "We traveled in a circus before we started to make Flying-Go-Rounds."

"Well, you've managed very nicely to tell them, my dear!" said Mr. Florabella. "The secret is out!" He nodded toward the children. "Flying-Go-Round Number 624."

"I still don't understand, so it might just as well be a secret," said Randy.

40

"Unless you mean that a Flying-Go-Round is a balloon basket," said Michael.

"No, not exactly. We don't generally travel around in circles, but a Flying-Go-Round does," Mr. Florabella answered, still speaking in riddles. He moved the tip of his umbrella clockwise around the circle on the paper that served as a picnic cloth. "Like this. Around and around."

"Some people call it a Merry-Go-Round," said Mrs. Florabella. "We had one in the circus. In Paris it was called a Carrousel."

"You make Merry-Go-Rounds!" said the children in delight.

"Flying-Go-Rounds," corrected Mr. Florabella. "The Florabella Flying-Go-Rounds. There is a difference. Let me explain. No, on second thought we had better put up the tent first. This ought to be discussed 'under the hat,' as the saying goes. We don't like airing our plans about at the start. Something always happens if we do."

"That's why we lured the cats away, remember?" said Mrs. Florabella brightly.

"Are you planning a circus?" said Michael eagerly.

"Not exactly. Why?" said Mr. Florabella.

"Because you said something about putting up a tent."

"Oh, that's only to make everything invisible," said Mr. Florabella. "It's that roll of sailcloth. You might fetch it, and the bundle of bamboo sticks."

Unrolled, the sailcloth was a happy surprise. It was cut in the shape of a large circle, blue on both sides, the color of the sky on a sunny day, but the outer side was also painted with green trees, bushes, and meadow flowers.

"It is a wigwam. We borrowed the idea from the Sioux Indians of Minnesota, U.S.A."

"It's absolutely beautiful," said Randy.

"I didn't know the Indians painted trees and bushes on their wigwams," said Michael.

"Usually they paint the sun and the moon and the stars, such things," said Mr. Florabella. "The trees were our idea. When you want to hide, where do you go? Behind the sun and the moon

41

and the stars? No, you take to the woods. You find a tree, the larger the better. A clump of bushes, or a forest. The wigwam must hide not only myself and Mrs. Florabella, but the balloon basket and the balloon as well."

"You are very clever," said Michael in admiration.

"I don't mind admitting it myself," said Mr. Florabella, well pleased. He untied the red-tasseled cord from the bundle of bamboo sticks. "I've painted the bamboo to look like birchwood. They're all marked *one, two, three,* and so on. Fitted together they make a center pole for the wigwam. You can learn a trick or two from me."

In no time at all he had the bamboo fitted together, the end of one stick inserted into the hollow end of the other. Then he and Michael pulled the painted sailcloth over the balloon basket.

"Now if you'll please crawl under the wigwam with the pole and then stand up, holding the pole in the center," Mr. Florabella said. "No, on second thought, I'll do it. I don't want you to be invisible just yet. There's still a bit of work to do. You can fetch the wooden stakes and the hammer."

"We couldn't find any wooden stakes or a hammer in Mira-Rami."

"I never use anything but a stone for a hammer, like the Indians," said Mr. Florabella, now invisible under the sailcloth. "Make stakes out of the firewood. Just sharpen the ends a little like arrowheads."

"I don't have a knife."

"Use the soup ladle instead," said Mrs. Florabella, opening the picnic basket.

"I don't think that will help much," Michael said, trying not to laugh.

"But we always use the soup ladle—the handle." Detached, the handle proved to be a bread knife, well sharpened. "We keep everything as compact as possible, to save space."

"Mind my fingers!" Mr. Florabella called out merrily from under the wigwam when Michael started pounding the stakes. "Mind my toes! Mind my head!"

42

"You are supposed to be invisible."

"Then mind your own fingers with that Indian club. When you have finished with it, tie the lower edge of the wigwam to the stakes with sinew thongs. Sailor's knots will do."

The sinew thongs looked to Michael and Randy more like old shoelaces.

"Tell me when you have finished," said Mr. Florabella, who was a little tired of being invisible. It was rather stuffy under the sailcloth.

Randy was no help at all. She tied everything in butterfly bows, and so did Mrs. Florabella, who said she didn't know how to make sailor's knots, or any knots at all.

"Then how do you sew?" asked Randy.

"Carolino sleeps in my sewing basket and tangles up the thread," Mrs. Florabella answered. "I only have to snip off a bit of thread for the needle. I always find a knot ready-made at the end of it."

Though still invisible, Mr. Florabella was now moving about under the sailcloth like Pushkin the bear, first on his hands and

knees and then standing upright, dancing about as he shifted
the center pole into position. Painted flowers, bushes, and then
tall trees seemed to spring up from the ground. The wigwam
stood in place. From whatever side you looked, it was a lovely
sight, a little round forest.

"How are you going to get out, Mr. Florabella?" said Randy.

"Through a hollow in a tree," he answered. "Watch and see!
Here I be!" He had invented the poem for the occasion. And
there he was, peering out of a painted tree trunk, like a wood-
pecker in its nest. It was the flap of the tent that had been hooked
shut from within. He ducked his head inside the tree trunk, but
presently the flap of the wigwam opened as though the painted
tree had split in half. There stood Mr. Florabella. He was wear-
ing over his bowler hat an Indian war-bonnet of wild-turkey
feathers, bluejay feathers, and an eagle feather at the center. He
was pretending to smoke a long-stemmed Indian peace pipe of
smooth red pipestone, adorned with more feathers. How he had
done it all so quickly, the children could not imagine.

"Welcome to the powwow," he said. He gave a loud Indian war
whoop, which Mrs. Florabella answered.

It was rather like a circus after all.

A Nearly Invisible Powwow

Within the wigwam it was like twilight and like dawn, whichever time you wanted to choose. It was a shadowed, secret place, though a little crowded at the moment. The Sky Bird took half the space. The net of ropes and the limp balloon hung over the side of the basket, forming a hammock lined with red silk. Mrs. Florabella had chosen the hammock to sit in, dangling her pink slippers above the ground. "I expect I'll fall asleep," she said, yawning. "It's just like a cradle."

Michael and Randy sat on the velvet cushions, because the coverings on the campstools looked a bit too moth-eaten. They were afraid they might tear them. Mr. Florabella was much too busy to sit down. He took off the feathered war-bonnet and put it in the balloon basket—reserve flying power. Then he opened the canvas satchel with a great show of importance.

"Attention, everyone! I am about to let out the animals."

"What animals?" said Randy, wondering what was going to happen.

"The animals in the satchel. Guess *what*."

"A rabbit," said Randy promptly. "Magicians always have a rabbit."

"Yes, but they usually pull it out of a hat instead of a satchel," said Mr. Florabella.

"Pigeons," said Randy. "Magicians also have pigeons."

"*Ordinary* magicians," said Mr. Florabella. "Think of something larger, more surprising."

45

"How about an elephant?" said Michael, thinking it a joke. "A baby elephant."

"Why not?" said Mr. Florabella.

"Or a giraffe."

"Here they come!" said Mr. Florabella, playing the clown. "The elephant first, and then the giraffe."

The satchel appeared to be filled with nothing but grimy, crumpled pieces of paper, the kind that Mr. O'Rafferty collected and sold. Mr. Florabella made a pretense of working a charm over them, gesturing and mumbling strange words in a very comic manner so that Michael and Randy could not help giggling. He even took out the bamboo spying-glass from the umbrella and played on it as though it were a flute.

"That's to charm them," he said, winking at the children. "They're wild animals, you see."

"It's almost as good as a circus," said Randy.

Mr. Florabella pulled two pieces of paper from the satchel. When unfolded they revealed colored-crayon drawings of an elephant and a giraffe. The baby elephant was almost as large as the balloon basket, and the giraffe reached as high as the pole of the wigwam. The elephant was gray with a red saddle cloth; the giraffe was yellow with dark brown spots and had a saddlecloth of bright green.

"Oh, pictures!" said the children, rather disappointed. "We thought at first they were going to be *real* ones."

"I must say they are very nicely drawn," Randy added, so as not to offend Mr. Florabella. "They *look* real."

"And they'll become quite real in time, that I can promise you," said Mr. Florabella. "Would you like to look at them through the spying-glass?"

The children took turns looking through the bamboo tube, exclaiming "Oh!" and "Ah!" while Mr. Florabella did a lot of explaining.

"They are for the Flying-Go-Round. Most everyone gets to ride a horse or a pony at one time or the other, even if it is only a rocking horse, or a little wooden pony on a Merry-Go-Round. But not everyone gets a chance to ride an elephant or a giraffe."

"I've always wanted to ride a camel," said Michael.

"I have one here, but I can't let it out of the satchel now. There's no room in the wigwam."

"I'd like to ride on the back of a goose or a swan," said Randy. "There's a story about a boy who rode on the back of a goose all over the world."

"If there isn't one already in the satchel, I'll put one there," said Mr. Florabella. "That's the whole idea of a Florabella Flying-Go-Round. Whatever bird or animal you wish to ride will be there. At least twelve of them, a good dozen. One for each number on the clock face. I do the animals. Mrs. Florabella does the saddlecloths, mostly red velvet ones."

48

"Where will the Flying-Go-Round be?" Michael asked. "And when?"

Randy had a few questions, too. "How long does it take to make a Flying-Go-Round? Will we pay to ride it? Will you take it away when you go, or are you going to stay here always?"

"Questions and answers, that's a game," said Mr. Florabella. "I know all the questions and I know all the answers, but not as quick as a canary can hop from the brim of a hat. First questions first. 'Where is the Flying-Go-Round going to be?' Usually we put it on a meadow surrounded by shady trees."

"There isn't any such place here," said the children.

"Or down in a dell or a hollow."

"Like Mira-Rami," said Randy. "Only it's mostly always filled up."

"There ought to be a meadow outside of every town and at least one *inside* the town, right in the center," said Mr. Florabella, raising his voice like an orator. "That's the way I'd plan a town. I've a good notion to tell that to the Burgomaster, or the Mayor, or the Governor, or whatever-his-name-is. In fact, I may be obliged to, though I don't like getting grownups mixed in with Flying-Go-Rounds. It isn't often that you find a grownup who understands these things—"

"Mr. O'Rafferty might," said Michael. "And he's always good at advice."

"Advice?" said Mr. Florabella suspiciously. "I never fancied grown-up advice."

"I don't think Mr. O'Rafferty is really a grownup," said Randy slowly. "He may be very old, but he still plays marbles and sails paper boats in a washtub, and once I saw him standing on his head."

"That sounds a little more hopeful. Who exactly is this Mr. O'Rafferty?"

"Mr. O'Rafferty," Michael said with dignity, "is our grandfather."

"Oh," said Mr. Florabella, and he looked rather embarrassed. "Your grandfather, did you say?"

49

After that no one said anything for a moment or two. Mrs. Florabella yawned loudly, awakening from sleep. "How still it is," she said with a listening look, sitting up in the hammock and putting her hat straight. "Not a sound anywhere. Not even a cat. That's one good thing about the avalanche. It frightened all the cats away."

"Sh!" whispered Mr. Florabella, cautioning her into silence. He, too, had a listening look, cocking his head to one side like a sparrow. It was so quiet that the rustling of the elderberry leaves could be heard above the wigwam, some of the branches scratching against the sailcloth. "I think one of the cats has come back. . . ."

He tiptoed over to the closed flap of the wigwam, and then with a quick gesture thrust it open.

And there, standing outside the wigwam, or rather stooping, with one ear pressed closely against the painted sailcloth, was Mr. O'Hara the policeman.

Behind Twelve Closed Doors

Mr. O'Hara looked rather red-faced and ashamed, caught listening.

"I was just making my rounds," he said. "And I noticed this tent—"

"Wigwam," Mr. Florabella corrected.

"All right, *wigwam*," said Mr. O'Hara. "I couldn't help admirmiring it."

"Thank you. I hope you don't mind our putting it here."

"Children have to play somewhere," said Mr. O'Hara, quite as though Mr. Florabella were a child in spite of his mustache and bowler hat. Mr. O'Hara himself had a mustache of the type known as "walrus," which perhaps made him feel superior. "That's the trouble with this town—no meadows, no playgrounds." He had indeed been listening! He looked at Mr. Florabella curiously. "You're a new boy, aren't you? I don't think I've seen you around before, not in that get-up anyway."

"Get-up? I don't understand."

"Costume," said Mr. O'Hara patiently. "Fancy dress and all that." He was looking in particular at Mr. O'Hara's mustache now. He seemed to suspect that it had been drawn above Mr. Florabella's mouth with charcoal or a burnt matchstick, or that at best it was a false carnival mustache, fixed there with glue or chewing gum. In fact, he said as much. "Do you use glue or chewing gum?"

"For what?" said Mr. Florabella.

"For your mustache."

"I use beeswax. The best possible quality."

Michael and Randy peered out of the wigwam rather anxiously.

"Oh, it's *you*, is it?" said Mr. O'Hara grinning. "What are you two up to now?"

"We're not up to anything," said Randy. "We were only invited to a powwow. Besides, we thought we were *invisible*."

"That's what children always think when they're up to mischief," said Mr. O'Hara, who had two children of his own. "They think they're invisible."

He peered into the wigwam but was too big to enter it. Besides, he had not been invited. Like most grownups he had a lot of questions to ask.

"What's in that satchel?"

"Paper," Michael said promptly. He and Randy were hurriedly folding the secret pictures of the elephant and giraffe. "Old paper. We're on our way to Mr. O'Rafferty's with it this very minute."

For once Mr. Florabella was silent. He let Michael and Randy answer all the questions.

"All right. I was only asking," said Mr. O'Hara. "I thought you might be on your way to the Burgomaster, or the Mayor, or the Governor, or whatever-his-name-is."

"He heard *everything*," Randy whispered in dismay.

In the twilight of the wigwam Mr. O'Hara now noticed Mrs. Florabella in the rope hammock with Carolino perched on her hat.

"Well, I never!" said Mr. O'Hara in surprise. "Real birds is it now! What will they think of next for fancy hats."

"That's Mrs. Florabella and Carolino," said Randy quickly. "And they're only sitting in the hammock."

"So I see. And what would there be in that big wash basket?"

"It's not a wash basket!" said Randy. "It's a—it's a nest."

"All right, it's a nest," said Mr. O'Hara. "A big nest for a little bird."

"Yes, isn't it?"

Mrs. Florabella said nothing at all, but swung back and forth in the hammock, looking rather frightened.

"Well, now," said Mr. O'Hara, "if you're off to Mr. O'Rafferty's, the lot of you, shall I be minding the wigwam while you're gone? Keep an eye on it, so to speak?"

"That is indeed kind of you, officer," said Mr. Florabella, politely doffing his hat.

Since there seemed nothing else to do but pay a visit to Mr. O'Rafferty, the four marched off to Shanty Town: Randy and Mrs. Florabella hand in hand; Mr. Florabella, carrying his purple umbrella; and Michael, carrying the canvas satchel.

"We're getting ourselves nicely mixed up with grownups," said Mr. Florabella. "First this police officer, and now Mr. O'Rafferty."

"I'm sorry," said Michael apologetically. "When Mr. O'Hara asked me about the satchel, I didn't know what else to say. I was afraid he would ask you to open it."

"Grownups are so inquisitive," said Mr. Florabella. "Always asking questions—"

"Mr. O'Hara thought you and Mrs. Florabella were children," said Randy. "Can you imagine that!"

"We consider it a compliment," said Mr. Florabella. "He couldn't have said anything nicer, even if he tried. Certainly we are the young in heart."

Mr. O'Rafferty was at the pump in Shanty Town when they arrived, still floating paper boats in a washtub. He could do this for hours, and since he collected old paper there was always enough for new boats when the others got too wet or ship-wrecked. He was a little man, red-faced, with sea-blue eyes and a head as smooth and bald as a gull's egg. When he walked he swayed from side to side as though he were on the deck of a schooner, bracing himself against the wind.

Though he had been a sailor, he knew a little about carpentry too. He had built the house in which they lived from the treasure-trove of Mira-Rami, and a very unusual house it was. A dozen or more wooden doors, nailed side by side, formed part of the walls, and very handy all those doorknobs were, useful as pegs for hanging things. The roof was made of broken tiles and bits of flowerpots; the chimney, of broken bricks, some red, some yellow, some brown. There was a little pavement outside the front door, made of more bricks and flagstones. It was a house with only one room, nearly square, but divided into sections with curtains of old sailcloth. The beds, the cupboard, the chairs, and the table were all fashioned out of packing cases, crates, and odds and ends of lumber which Mr. O'Rafferty said was driftwood. The stove that warmed them in winter and cooked the food at all seasons had come from the Iron Mountain of Mira-Rami, and so had every nail in the house and in the furniture as well. There was not a cup or a plate or a bowl that did not have a crack or chip in it, or a pot or a pan that had not been mended by the iron-monger. It was all flotsam and jetsam, said Mr. O'Rafferty with pride.

When Michael and Randy told him that the Florabellas had come on secret business, Mr. O'Rafferty at once suggested a meeting in the little house, behind closed doors, which meant a dozen or more closed doors.

The Florabellas were enchanted with the house. "It's just the kind of house we'd like to have if we ever settle down," they said. "Which we won't, since flying has become a habit."

"At first I couldn't settle my sea legs down in one place, but now I've nearly succeeded," said Mr. O'Rafferty. "The doors help. With twelve of them, I always have the feeling there is a way of escape, an invitation to adventure."

Mr. O'Rafferty had such a round, kind, smiling face that he inspired confidence at once. "Now," he said, after the idea of the Flying-Go-Round had been discussed, "let's have a look at the plans." He put on his wire spectacles and studied the paper Mr. Florabella took from the satchel. "What an amazing contraption!"

"Contraption?" said Mr. Florabella.

"Yes, a contraption. I can't make head or tail out of it. Any invention as clever and complicated, as strange and bewildering as this is a contraption. I congratulate you!"

"Thank you."

"And all run on wind and air, you say. Balloons, kites, fringes and feathers, fans and flags. Amazing! Why it's half sister to a sailboat! I once had an idea for a land boat, also run by air—"

"There is a secret use of a turning wheel at the center," said Mr. Florabella. "Hidden, of course—under a canopy. That's to start it off on quiet days when there's no wind blowing. A kind of perpetual-motion idea."

"Clockwork precision," said Mr. O'Rafferty, nodding.

"Exactly," said Mr. Florabella, twirling his watch in a circular motion.

"Where do you aim to set it up?"

"That is the problem. There isn't any meadow."

"There was one once," said Mr. O'Rafferty, taking off his spectacles, "when I was a boy. Green in summer, with the wind blowing across it like it was a sea of grass. That's how I got my first idea of being a sailor. There was a lovely dell, Dingle Dell, it was called, green as a shamrock. It's that place my grandchildren call the Land of Mira-Rami. That's the most likely spot now, only we'd have to cart away all the rubbish first."

"That would change Mira-Rami," said Michael, seriously. "Carting away everything—"

"It would make a big valley out of it, that's all," said Mr. O'Rafferty. "And in time it would be green again like Dingle Dell. You'd not be regretting that, once you'd seen it."

"But that's the way we always see it," said Randy. "Green. Especially through the Florabellas' spying-glass."

"I hope this won't mean a visit to the Mayor and the town council," said Mr. Florabella, frowning. "We've had that problem before. This isn't the first Flying-Go-Round we've set up, you know. It's Number 624."

"No need to see the town council yet," said Mr. O'Rafferty. "Not with Mr. O'Hara on your side."

"Are you sure he's on our side?" said Mr. Florabella. "He doesn't know anything about it yet."

"That's why he's on your side," said Mr. O'Rafferty, winking. "He doesn't know anything yet. Anyway, Mr. O'Hara and the town council should be glad to get rid of all that rubbish."

"Where are we going to put the rubbish?" said Michael.

"What do you suggest, Mr. Florabella?" said Mr. O'Rafferty.

"Usually we fill up some other holes or hollows. That is if they need filling."

"Then I'll put a little notice for you outside our house: HOLES FILLED UP—GRATIS," said Mr. O'Rafferty.

"What is 'gratis'?" asked Randy.

"That means 'free,' without pay."

"We always charged a small fee," said Mr. Florabella. "For the general fund, to help things get started. Paint for the wooden animals, the saddlecloths, that sort of thing, you know."

"All right," said Mr. O'Rafferty. "I'll just change the sign to read PARTLY GRATIS. In that way the customers will be getting *something* for nothing, but not everything."

"What part will they get for nothing?" said Randy, who wanted things clear in her mind.

"Why I expect they'll be getting the material free, the rubbish."

"That's right," said Mr. Florabella. "All they pay us for is the work, the trouble of carting the rubbish."

"Who is going to do all the carting?" asked Michael, a little worried.

"We've never had any problem there," said Mr. Florabella. "You see, there are twelve animals in each Flying-Go-Round, birds or animals, whatever you choose. So naturally there are twelve riders, which means twelve children. Once you tell a dozen children they are invited to share a secret, each child himself will provide a dozen or more helpers. No, the problem, if there is one, would be *too many* helpers."

"I'd like to have a look at those animals," said Mr. O'Rafferty. "That menagerie you have in the satchel. What have you got?"

"Why, most anything at all," said Mr. Florabella. "Creatures, great and small. Creatures with wings, and creatures without wings, so swift they might well have hidden wings. Horses with winged hoofs and flying manes, of course. But have you ever seen a squirrel flying from one branch of a tree to another? A deer leaping? A rabbit running? They all know the language of the wind."

"A flying fish, a dolphin sporting in the sea," said Mr. O'Rafferty. "They can tell you a thing or two about wings as well." He had put on his spectacles again and was peering at the drawings Mr. Florabella was unfolding.

"They're a bit rumpled," said Mr. Florabella.

"Dear me, yes!" said Mr. O'Rafferty. "Rumpled and crumpled. They must be ironed."

"Mrs. Florabella used to do it from time to time, but the iron got too sooty over an open fire."

"I once ruined a white swan," said Mrs. Florabella, giggling. "It turned quite black."

"And no real loss," said Mr. O'Rafferty. "I've seen them in Australia. Black swans with red beaks."

Although the day was warm, Mr. O'Rafferty stoked a fire in the cookstove and put a flatiron on to heat and a leaky tea-kettle on to boil.

"We'll have a spot of tea, outdoors if you like, in the sunshine. I want to use the floor as an ironing board."

"We've just *had* tea," said Randy.

"It's always teatime," said Mr. Florabella, looking at his watch.

Mr. O'Rafferty and Michael and Randy began shoving all the furniture against the twelve closed doors, and then they spread out the animal drawings on the floor. The Florabellas, as usual, did nothing but just watched. The flatiron was hot long before the water in the leaky tea-kettle, which had to be constantly refilled.

"I'm enjoying this," said Mr. O'Rafferty, crawling on the floor on his hands and knees. "It's a pleasure to iron out wrinkles and turn frowns into smiles."

His own face, round and smiling, did not show a wrinkle. Nor did the faces of the Florabellas or Michael or Randy. They were all smiling happily. On the brim of the marvelous velvet hat Carolino was singing.

Partly Gratis

Mr. O'Rafferty, true to his word, put up a notice on his front door: HOLES FILLED UP—PARTLY GRATIS. So for a day or two he and Michael and Randy were very busy. There were a good many holes in Shanty Town that needed filling—mostly in roofs and chimneys, and knotholes in the boards in the walls. However, they were small holes that used only a few tiles, broken flowerpots, bricks, and bits of wood from Mira-Rami. During all the activity the Florabellas were nearly always invisible in the wigwam. They played chess and checkers and other indoor games on the red-and-white tablecloth, now rescued from the valley. The dust of Mira-Rami bothered Mrs. Florabella, so when she came out of the wigwam she often put a clothespin on her nose. In that way she could not breathe the dust. Carolino thought it was meant as a new perch. This embarrassed Mrs. Florabella, since everyone believed she was playing the clown.

To use more bricks and stones Mr. O'Rafferty decided to make pavements and verandas outside the houses of Shanty Town as well as a large paved square around the pump. This was a great improvement in Shanty Town, which had always been muddy in wet weather and dusty in dry weather. But in Mira-Rami there was hardly any change at all, even though Michael and Randy and the other children of Shanty Town removed cartloads of bricks and stones. The hills became a little smaller, the valley a little wider, but not so you could really notice it. In that way it was discouraging. There were still mountains of rubbish.

No one in Shanty Town understood the idea of *Partly Gratis*. In Shanty Town people had always traded things, so no one wanted to pay a fee. Michael and Randy got only a few pennies here and there. Mr. Florabella, fishing from the rim of the Pudding Basin with his magnetized umbrella, caught some pennies himself. "Fishing for goldfish" he called it, a lazy but pleasant pastime. Taffy and the other cats who had been frightened away by the avalanche now came back to Mira-Rami, one by one. Mr. Florabella was obliged to fish for sardine tins too, to keep the cats from Carolino.

"Why don't you just put Carolino in the bird cage?" Michael suggested. "You'd have more time to help us with the rubbish."

"Don't let Mrs. Florabella hear you say that!" said Mr. Florabella, horrified. "How would you like being in a bird cage?"

"But I'm not a bird," said Michael.

"Well, any cage at all. Everyone likes to feel free, wings or not."

"Then why do you have a bird cage with you?" asked Michael. "I saw it the day we unloaded the luggage."

"We use the cage for an entirely different purpose," said Mr. Florabella mysteriously. "Which you will see in time."

"If you like birds so much, how did you get the feather in your hat?" one of the boys of Shanty Town dared to ask. He was little Larry Lee with a quick tongue.

"From a woodcock," said Mr. Florabella. "I saved him from the hunter's gun by blowing a whistle. I had sighted the hunters with my spying-glass. Later I found the feather lying on the ground. I accepted it as a token of appreciation."

"And Mrs. Florabella's pink ostrich plumes," said Randy. "I've been meaning to ask her about them."

"I once designed a marvelous ostrich for the Flying-Go-Round. The ostrich I used as a model was so pleased with the likeness that Mrs. Florabella was presented with a number of plumes."

"I didn't know that ostriches had pink plumes," said Larry Lee suspiciously.

"They were originally white, but they turned pink while we were flying through a tropical sunset."

"A likely story," said Larry Lee.

61

"Why not?" said Randy. "If you stay in the sun long enough you turn not only pink but red."

"Exactly," said Mr. Florabella gratefully.

All this chatter was interesting, but it did not help to load the three-wheeled cart with rubbish. However, there were no more holes in Shanty Town to be filled, nor was there any more ground to pave with bricks and stones.

At the end of the third day Mr. O'Rafferty's round face had a wrinkle or two that had never been there before. He had been doing a lot of thinking. He went over to Mira-Rami to visit the Florabellas in the wigwam. Mrs. Florabella was swinging in the hammock, and Mr. Florabella was drawing animal pictures with colored crayons—designs for the Flying-Go-Round.

"No more holes," said Mr. O'Rafferty. "We'll have to change the sign. It ought to read MOUNTAINS BUILT TO ORDER—ALL SIZES."

"That's more like it!" Mr. Florabella said. "Now we're getting somewhere!"

It was a brilliant idea. Hardly had the notice been posted on the door when there were two projects under way. Old Mr. Kelly said he was tired of the view from his window. He would like some mountain scenery to hide the factories and smokestacks. Either the Rocky Mountains or the Alps would do.

"The Rocky Mountains, no," said Mr. O'Rafferty. "We used the last of the rocks for the pavement around the pump. How about a mountain range rich in metal? Tin, for instance, and a good, thick vein of iron. You might like to do a little mining one day." Mr. Kelly thought it would be all right, though he had rather fancied the Rocky Mountains.

Mrs. O'Toole no sooner heard that Mr. Kelly was having mountain scenery than she decided she wanted some too. Green Mountains, White Mountains, and some Alps with edelweiss.

"No sooner said than done," said Mr. O'Rafferty cheerfully. "However, you may have to wait a day or two for them to turn green, but green they'll be I promise! A good sprinkling of grass seed and a light rainfall, and you'll think you're in Ireland."

For Mrs. O'Toole's White Mountains they would use the

broken china and crockery of Mira-Rami and part of the Diamond Glacier. The edelweiss was a problem because Mr. O'Rafferty, being a seaman, did not know what an edelweiss was, nor did he dare ask Mrs. O'Toole.

"I've always fancied an edelweiss," she said. "Ever since my sister's daughter sent me a post card from Switzerland. She got a fine job there, chambermaid in a hotel right on top of a mountain."

"It's a kind of mountain goat, I expect," Mr. O'Rafferty said to the Florabellas.

"Certainly not!" said Mr. Florabella. "An edelweiss is a white flower that grows in rocky places. We've seen them in the Alps as we flew over in our balloon."

"How about a white daisy?" said Mr. O'Rafferty. "I'll have Randy plant one from Mira-Rami in a flowerpot and set it on Mrs. O'Toole's mountain."

"Oh, no!" said Mrs. Florabella. "An edelweiss is more like a star, and it feels quite like white velvet. I'll make one for Mrs. O'Toole. All I need is a bit of velvet and my scissors."

It was the first work Mrs. Florabella had done in days. Mr. O'Rafferty could not help saying that the Florabellas were rather lazy, but they were to be forgiven since the idea of the Flying-Go-Round was theirs and they were thus supplying the brains. From sunup to sundown Michael and Randy and dozens of small helpers carted rubbish to Shanty Town. They used not only the three-wheeled cart but carried tin cans and broken crockery in baskets, shopping bags, and old washtubs. They even transplanted the green pumpkin so that they might use the baby carriage. Like the cart, the carriage had only three wheels. Mr. Florabella, fishing for copper pennies from the rim of the Pudding Basin, lazily watched the children at their work.

"Why don't you put the two front wheels at the back of the baby carriage, and the back wheel at the front, right in the middle like the wheel on a wheelbarrow?" he said. "You'll have better balance, and it'll be much easier to push. I'm surprised that Mr. O'Rafferty never thought of it. You might tell him that."

63

They delivered the message to Mr. O'Rafferty, who was supervising the mountain building in Shanty Town.

"Mr. O'Rafferty said he'd rather wait for a fourth wheel," Michael said when they returned. "Especially since there's all the time in the world. He doesn't like three-wheeled baby carriages or carts. Also he said if you'll take care of the winging wings he'll take care of the wheeling wheels."

"Fair enough," said Mr. Florabella meekly. "Anyway, if you find any extra fourth wheels, I'll need one for the Flying-Go-Round. I always put a wheel in the center—a very large one."

Mr. Florabella did stop his fishing the day the cookstove plateau was moved from the Iron Mountain. It was intended as the vein of iron for Mr. Kelly's new mountain. Michael and Randy had already taken out the biscuit tin with its treasure of jewels that had been hidden in the oven. They carried the box to Shanty Town, and Randy put it under her bed. Now the heavy, squat legs of the stove were tied with rope, and every child from Shanty Town was trying to move the stove up the rim of the Pudding Basin, all of them pulling and tugging. Mr. Florabella came to the rescue, pointing the magnetized umbrella at the oven door. The tip of the umbrella got stuck to the oven and Mr. Florabella with it, gripping the carved ivory handle. So it was difficult to tell if he was any help at all.

In Shanty Town Mr. O'Rafferty greeted the arrival with cheers of welcome.

64

"Here comes your vein of iron," he called out to Mr. Kelly, who was looking at the changing view from his window. Ever since the first cartload of tin cans had arrived, Mr. Kelly had not left the window. Likewise Mr. O'Toole was watching her growing mountain of crockery. Both Mr. Kelly and Mrs. O'Toole were rather worried.

"But these are only the foundations," Mr. O'Rafferty kept repeating. "We'll cover everything nicely with dust and dirt, sprinkle grass seed on it, and in no time at all you'll have lovely mountain scenery. I've already told you that."

Mr. Kelly climbed out of his window to inspect the vein of iron.

"Where will you have it, Mr. Kelly? In the heart of the mountain, or just set down midway like a nice cozy plateau?"

"I don't know as I want it covered up," said Mr. Kelly, peering into the oven and poking the rusty grate with his cane. "I rather fancy this stove. I don't think I want to go mining for it, not when it's already dug up and mined."

"Well, you just think about it for a little," said Mr. O'Rafferty. "It'll give these mountain builders a chance to rest a bit." And to Mrs. O'Toole he said encouragingly, "Your edelweiss is coming along just fine. We'll be planting it soon along with the grass seed."

All these days, while the holes in Shanty Town were being filled and the stone-and-brick pavements laid, Mr. O'Hara, the policeman, had gone about with one eye shut, and sometimes with both

eyes shut, pretending not to notice anything. It had almost become a habit with Mr. O'Hara, quite as though a gigantic wigwam had been set up, making everything invisible. But, now, suddenly Mr. O'Hara was there in Shanty Town with both eyes wide open.

"What's all this?" he said. He was pointing to Mr. Kelly's mountain, and Mrs. O'Toole's mountain, and all the little foothills. "Who is responsible for this?"

Mr. O'Rafferty was not being responsible. Neither was Mr. Florabella. They made themselves very small and disappeared behind Mr. O'Rafferty's twelve closed doors.

"I knew it!" Mr. O'Rafferty whispered. "It was too good to be true."

"We'd better keep out of it," said Mr. Florabella. "Mr. O'Hara seems partial to children. They'll do better without us."

"Cart all this junk back to the Dump Yard," roared Mr. O'Hara.

"All of it?" the childen said in dismay.

"That's what I said! All of it!"

66

"The stove too?" Michael asked. "It took us all morning to get it here."

"Everything!" said Mr. O'Hara.

"Not the stove," said Mr. Kelly. "I fancy that stove. I could do a little outdoor cooking on it. There's nothing like home-cooked outdoor food for the appetite. My appetite has been right poorly lately, Mr. O'Hara."

"All right, keep the stove," said Mr. O'Hara. "But that's all! Why there are *mountains* of rubbish here!"

"That's what we were trying to make," said Randy, near tears. "Mountains . . ."

"I'm sorry about this," said Mr. O'Hara, more kindly. He shook his head. "What you need is a nice green meadow where all of you could play—"

"But that's what we were trying to make out of Mira—out of the Dump Yard," said Randy. She had never said the word before, never called Mira-Rami the "Dump Yard," and saying so now seemed a betrayal of everything good she had ever imagined or dreamed about. She burst into tears.

"Now, now," said Mr. O'Hara unhappily. "Things have come to a pretty pass indeed, if brave little girls begin to cry."

"She's not really crying," said Michael. "She's only tired. If you knew how many cartloads of rubbish—"

"We'll have to get you a meadow somehow," said Mr. O'Hara with resolution. "We'll all go to the Mayor and have a chat with him. There doesn't seem to be anything else to do."

His Honor the Mayor

"Who are these people?" said the Mayor. He was fat, round, and well fed, but in spite of this not at all jovial. He was seated in a high-backed chair at an oaken table, and with him were his twelve councilmen.

"They're the children of Shanty Town, Your Honor," said Mr. O'Hara respectfully. "Also Mr. O'Rafferty, Mr. Kelly, Mrs. O'Toole—"

"Yes, yes, so I see. I mean the other two, the ones in fancy dress," said the Mayor, pointing to the Florabellas. "The dwarfs."

Whether Mr. and Mrs. Florabella had ever been called dwarfs before, they did not say. They did not look very pleased. Their bright, birdlike eyes flashed, they straightened their shoulders, and stood on tiptoes to appear taller.

"They used to be in a traveling circus," said Mr. O'Hara.

"It looks like they still are," said the Mayor rudely.

"They are the famous Florabellas," said Mr. O'Hara.

"I wouldn't know," said the Mayor. "Anyway, why have you come?"

"It's about a meadow," said Mr. O'Hara. "The one outside Shanty Town—"

"Well, what about it?" said the Mayor impatiently.

"It isn't there any more, Your Honor."

"What do you mean, it isn't there any more. Where has it gone?"

68

"That's what we all want to ask *you*," said Mr. O'Hara.

"What's all this rigamarole?" said the Mayor. "I didn't take your meadow."

"Someone did," said Mr. O'Hara staunchly. "Mr. O'Rafferty here can tell you that there was a meadow there once."

"That's right, Your Honor," said Mr. O'Rafferty. "It was a lovely green meadow with sheep and cows grazing on it. And there used to be a Horse Fair twice a year and gypsy caravans. And what have you done with it? Why you've pulled out every blade of grass and every tree and left nothing but dust and dirt. The same thing with Dingle Dell. Even worse, I might say. It was a green hollow of trees and ferns, a joy to see. And what have you done with it? Filled it up with rubbish, made a Dump Yard out of it!"

"What can I do about it?" said the Mayor, feeling rather uncomfortable with the eyes of Mr. O'Rafferty, Mr. O'Hara, the Florabellas, and all the children of Shanty Town looking at him—as well as Mr. Kelly and Mrs. O'Toole, who were great starers. "It was done a long time ago."

"Not so long as all that!" said Mr. O'Rafferty. "We're only asking that you put it back again the way it was. A most reasonable request. Clear out the rubbish, sprinkle grass seed, plant a few trees, and let nature take care of the rest. In fact, we'll do it ourselves if you give us the permission."

"It's quite impossible," said the Mayor. "It's the Dump Yard. Every town has a Dump Yard."

"It seems you think more of rubbish than you do of children," said Mr. O'Rafferty, both sad and angry. "They have no place to play—"

"It's only a suggestion, Your Honor," said Mr. O'Hara politely, "but couldn't there be a Dump Yard a little farther out of the town, not so near Shanty Town—"

"If the ocean were here we could dump everything into it," said Mr. O'Rafferty. "The biggest hole I ever saw was the ocean. It could swallow the Dump Yard like a peppermint lozenge. It would just melt in its mouth and disappear."

69

"The way I see it," said the Mayor, "you're wasting my time and that of the town council with a lot of rubbish. Yes, just a lot of rubbish!"

There was a very large silence. Everyone looked at the Mayor, shocked and surprised. Even the councilmen seemed uncomfortable. No one said anything at all, but there was a great sigh of disappointment from all the unhappy children. It sounded like the red balloon when the last breath of air was being drained out of it. Then unexpectedly there was a bird call, loud and impertinent, much too saucy to be that of a canary. It was undoubtedly little Larry Lee, though Carolino took the blame for it. Up to now Carolino had been as quiet and still as a gold ornament upon Mrs. Florabella's marvelous hat.

"What was that?" said the Mayor sharply. "Did I hear a note of disrespect?"

"That was Carolino," said Mrs. Florabella sweetly, but looking rather frightened. She pointed with a gloved hand to the rim of her hat. "Our pet canary—"

"Oh, a bird act, is it?" said the Mayor. "Circus tricks!"

"Oh, no!" said Mrs. Florabella. "We don't travel in the circus any more. We make Flying-Go-Rounds."

"Something like Merry-Go-Rounds," Michael said quickly. "Only different—"

"That's the other reason why we're here," said Mr. O'Hara. "That's why we need a meadow."

"Ah!" said the Mayor as though he had discovered some dark and dreadful secret. "So that's it, is it? You want a meadow so these Florabellas can set up a carnival! Only you're using these children as an excuse—"

"Not at all!" interrupted Mr. Florabella. He came forward with his umbrella and satchel. He noticeably neglected to say "Your Honor." "The children are the *reason*, not the *excuse!* The Florabella Flying-Go-Rounds are entirely for children. We don't accept a pennyworth of profit. We only set up a Flying-Go-Round, see that it is in good flying order, and then we depart."

The Mayor stared at Mr. Florabella in disbelief, scratching his

70

head as though in deep throught. "You set up this Merry-Go-Round or whatever it is, and then you just go off and leave it?"

"Yes, exactly," said Mr. Florabella. "It is a present we make to children."

"Something is wrong somewhere," said the Mayor in bewilderment.

"It's a hobby of Mrs. Florabella and myself. We've already set up six hundred and twenty-three Flying-Go-Rounds in different parts of the world, in different countries. It doesn't seem to matter where we put them, they're always a success. I suppose it's because children everywhere have nearly the same dreams and hopes, and our Flying-Go-Rounds just add a little reality to those dreams, if you know what I mean."

"No, I don't know what you mean," said the Mayor.

"It's very simple really. You can't keep your feet on the ground twenty-four hours of the day and be happy. You must lift them off the ground once in a while and rest them on a cloud. In other words, dream a little. Once you get your feet off the ground, you'll be surprised what pleasant ideas and fancies come to you. Our Flying-Go-Rounds are designed to help all that. You'll find yourself riding on the back of a white swan, for instance, or through the desert on a camel. We have deer and gazelles for forest flying, as well as red and gray squirrels. Elephants, if you fancy the jungle."

Mr. Florabella opened his satchel and began taking out the colored drawings which had been ironed smooth by Mr. O'Rafferty and neatly folded.

"Cloud cuckoo," said the Mayor.

"Yes, isn't it?" said a little man who was an alderman, a member of the town council. "Delightful!" His name was Mr. Scroggins and he had a certain twinkle in his eyes that made one suspect he was not entirely grown-up.

"Here is the plan of the Flying-Go-Round," said Mr. Florabella, unfolding a square of paper. "You see, there is a center pole surmounted by a huge turning wheel, twelve spokes, to be exact. You might say it is the frame for the canopy. On the outer rim of

71

the wheel we tie ropes which support the flying animals on which the children ride. Though actually they sit in little upholstered boxes, and the painted wooden animals are attached to the sides of the boxes. However, it's quite the same as if the children were astride a bird or animal, without any danger at all of falling off."

The Mayor was looking at the plans with a very puzzled expression on his face. All the twelve members of the town council were looking too, peering over the round shoulders of the Mayor.

"Why, you haven't even got a platform here, have you?" said the Mayor explosively. "Not even a good solid floor to the thing!"

"Certainly not!" said Mr. Florabella. "The whole idea is to get your feet *off* the ground. That means the animals and birds as well. You don't think they're really going to fly if they keep their feet on the ground, do you? That's the main difference between a Flying-Go-Round and a Merry-Go-Round."

"Admirable!" said Mr. Scroggins, smiling and nodding his head. "Also amazing!"

"Admirable my foot!" said the Mayor, who was, at the same moment, stamping his foot impatiently. "Why the whole idea is not only cloud cuckoo, it's impossible! This plan doesn't make sense even for a contraption! This is nothing but a tomfoolery, and a nonsensical nonsense. Besides that, it won't work!"

"It *has* worked," said Mr. Florabella. "Six hundred and twenty-three Flying-Go-Rounds still running on their own power."

"Which is *what?*" said the Mayor.

"Flying power," said Mr. Florabella. "But that is something you would never understand. I'd only be wasting my time trying to explain it to you. In fact, in all the time I've wasted here, I could have set up another six hundred and twenty-three Flying-Go-Rounds somewhere else."

For Mr. Florabella to admit that he had wasted time was indeed a proof of his disgust and impatience—he, who carried a watch without hands! He took the animal drawings from the council table and stuffed them into the satchel without bothering to fold them. It looked very much as though the visit to the Mayor was finished.

73

"Don't forget *this*," said the Mayor, waving the plan of the Flying-Go-Round in the air like a flag. "For this silly business you want me to clear away the rubbish from the Dump Yard, do you? Well, it stays there, do you hear? Every last tin can and broken bottle!"

"I've met grown-up obstinacy and rudeness before in my travels," said Mr. Florabella, closing his satchel, "but never quite as bad as this!" He lifted his bowler hat and bowed. "Good day to you, Mr. Mayor. There's no need to tell you to keep your feet on the ground. There's nothing I know of that would lift them. No, not even my Flying-Go-Rounds, the lot of them. You couldn't fly with a thousand eagle wings sprouting from your shoulders. You've never even begun to dream! Why I doubt that you were ever a child. You were born grown-up. I can't think of anything worse that could ever happen to a person."

And with that final speech, Mr. Florabella turned and walked out of the Council Hall, and with him all the children of Shanty Town followed by Mrs. Florabella, Mrs. O'Toole, Mr. Kelly, Mr. O'Rafferty and, last of all, Mr. O'Hara the policeman.

Ways and Means

"That was a right brave speech," said Mr. O'Hara when he came out of the Town Hall. "But it didn't exactly win over the Mayor."

"I was sorry I had to make it," said Mr. Florabella. "It's the last speech on my list. I only use it in extreme cases."

"We had a try anyway, if that's any comfort to us," said Mr. O'Rafferty. He was frowning and he could almost feel the wrinkles on his face. He would have to begin ironing them out, as well as those on the faces of everyone else. Carolino alone seemed cheerful, hopping about on the brim of Mrs. Florabella's hat, chirping and warbling, trying to put everyone in good spirits.

"The pity of it!" said Mrs. O'Toole to Mr. Kelly. "I don't mind them taking away our mountains as much as I mind them taking away that meadow and turning it into a Dump Yard again. On account of the children and that flying contraption."

"Mr. Florabella! Just a moment, please!" It was Mr. Scroggins the alderman, hurrying out of the Town Hall. "Don't give up yet!"

"I don't intend to give up," said Mr. Florabella with courage. "Do you think I would disappoint these children? There are always ways and means even when things *look* hopeless."

"I'm glad to hear you say that," said Mr. Scroggins. "That's what I wanted to say myself: *There are always ways and means.*"

"Such as what?" said Mr. O'Rafferty with a glimmer of hope.

"Yes, such as what?" repeated Mr. O'Hara.

75

"Is there some place where we could talk?" said Mr. Scroggins in a low voice. "Behind closed doors?"

"Behind twelve closed doors if you like," said Mr. O'Rafferty. "I know just the place. In fact, I live in it."

"You see, I know a bit about the law," said Mr. Scroggins, winking. "I ought to, since I happen to be a lawyer."

"Will you be having any use for this?" said Randy going up to Mr. Scroggins. She was holding in both hands a square biscuit tin, very rusty. "We were going to give it to the Mayor, but he wasn't at all nice."

"What have we here?" said Mr. Scroggins, smiling.

"Jewels," said Randy, removing the lid from the tin box. "Our treasure. Michael and I thought the Mayor could buy a new Dump Yard somewhere else."

Mr. Scroggins and everyone else had a look in the box, in particular Mr. O'Hara who was very curious.

"Mostly sapphires, rubies, and emeralds," said Randy proudly. "We've polished them with pumice stone to take off the rough edges. They shine beautifully if you hold them up in the sun."

"So I see," said Mr. Scroggins and he held up a very large ruby to catch the light. Not for a moment did he or anyone think of saying that it looked like a bit of church-window glass. "A pity the Mayor and the councilmen didn't see this!"

"There wasn't a chance," said Randy. "We couldn't get a word in edgewise."

"Perhaps it's just as well," said Mr. Scroggins. "The light in the Town Hall is very poor. Your jewels might not have shown to advantage."

"Will there be enough to buy a new Dump Yard?"

"I don't rightly know," said Mr. Scroggins. "But I'll make a note of it." He took out a little black notebook from his pocket and wrote in it: *Jewels for new Dump Yard or meadow.* "Are you quite certain you want to give them away, all of them?"

"Yes, I think so," Randy said, "if we are certain to have the Flying-Go-Round. I'd like to save just a small ruby, no bigger

76

than a crumb, in case I should ever have a gold locket like Mrs. Florabella's."

"I'll make a note of that, too," said Mr. Scroggins. "And your name?"

"Miranda O'Rafferty. Only everyone calls me Randy."

"You ought to be putting that treasure in a safe place in the meantime," said Mr. O'Hara, smiling.

"We used to keep it in Mr. Kelly's oven when the stove was in Mira—in the Dump Yard, I mean."

"I'll be glad to oblige you," said Mr. Kelly.

"Oh, we've already found a secret place for it—behind twelve closed doors," said Randy. "Thank you all the same."

What happened behind Mr. O'Rafferty's twelve closed doors the children of Shanty Town did not know, for they were not invited to the meeting, not even Michael and Randy. Mr. Scroggins was of the opinion that since grownups had taken away the meadow and filled Dingle Dell with rubbish, it was only fitting and proper that grownups should try to make things right again. Everyone in Shanty Town agreed. The children all waited outside the O'Rafferty house, and though they peered into the twelve keyholes they saw nothing but sailcloth curtains, and though they pressed their ears against the outer walls they heard nothing but a murmur of voices, and then finally chuckles and loud laughter.

Mr. O'Rafferty opened the main door. He was smiling, all his wrinkles gone. Then out came Mr. Scroggins, Mr. O'Hara, and the Florabellas. They, too, were smiling.

"Well then, I'm relying on you to go ahead with the plans as quickly as possible," said Mr. Scroggins, shaking hands with the Florabellas. "If there is anything else I can do to help, please call on me. I'll do my very best."

"Are we going to have the Flying-Go-Round?" asked the waiting children hopefully.

"Yes, indeed, you are going to have your Flying-Go-Round," said Mr. Florabella, while Mrs. Florabella smiled and nodded. "We'll not leave before then, that we promise you!"

77

If he said anything else no one heard him, for all the children of Shanty Town were cheering.

Though the Florabellas often said they had all the time in the world, they were not wasting any of it now. They hurried about the rim of the Pudding Basin without a complaint about dust on black patent-leather shoes and pink satin slippers. Mr. Florabella pointed his umbrella here and there and everywhere, shouting orders to a regiment of workers, while Mrs. Florabella smiled and nodded encouragement.

It was in the Dump Yard, or rather the Land of Mira-Rami, once known as Dingle Dell, that the Flying-Go-Round was being built. This was perhaps where the Florabellas had always intended it to be built. They knew from the very beginning that there was no meadow near Shanty Town. Flying over the Dump Yard, they had seen the deep hollow in the ground, not as a place where rubbish was dumped, but as a green country of mountains and valleys—just as Michael and Randy always saw it, through the eyes of imagination. The bamboo spying-glass had made the promise of beauty a little clearer and brighter in the mind, that was all.

A light rain had fallen in the night, just enough to settle the dust of Mira-Rami and to encourage the weeds and vines to put out new leaves. In the morning Mira-Rami looked faintly green again, as though spring had come back in midsummer. The mountains that had been carried over to Shanty Town had been returned to Mira-Rami. They were arranged now only around the rim of the Pudding Basin, leaving a valley broad and wide as a meadow. Here the center pole of the Flying-Go-Round would rise. Mr. O'Rafferty called it a mainmast, as though it belonged to a sailboat. He was making it out of the "driftwood" of Mira-Rami—fence-posts and logs, strengthened with coils of wire and lengths of iron pipe. This was not as simple a trick as the bamboo sticks that formed the center pole of the wigwam, but up went the mainmast nevertheless.

Mr. Scroggins the alderman was responsible for some of the hurry and bustle. "The sooner the Flying-Go-Round is finished the better—before the Mayor gets wise to it," he said.

"Doesn't the Mayor know?" Michael and Randy asked, for Mr. O'Rafferty had told them nothing of the secret meeting behind the twelve closed doors.

"If he did I expect he'd be here now," said Mr. Scroggins. "But no one is telling him. Anyway, if I remember rightly, he didn't say 'Yes' and he didn't say 'No.' He only said, 'It won't work!' and 'The Dump Yard stays where it is!' "

"Oh," said Michael and Randy, not knowing much more than they did before, but feeling cheerful, nevertheless, because Mr. Scroggins was so cheerful.

Whenever Mr. Scroggins appeared, Mr. Florabella made a great show of looking at his watch quite as though it had hands. This was to impress Mr. Scroggins with the fact that everything was running like clockwork.

"People sometimes think Mrs. Florabella and I are lazy," said Mr. Florabella. "This is only because we give others a chance to work if it pleases them. We've built so many Flying-Go-Rounds we could do it blindfolded. But we know that children enjoy something more when they help build it themselves. It takes a little longer, that's all."

There was truth in what he said. The children went about laughing and singing, making play out of work. There were grownups besides Mr. O'Rafferty, Mr. O'Hara, and Mr. Scroggins who helped too. The Florabellas had to admit that certain grown-ups, the kind known as "the young in heart," were very nice. Everyone had something important to do on Project 624. Mr. Kelly and Mrs. O'Toole helped the youngest children to gather flying power that would be used in the red velvet cushions and upholstery of the riding boxes. This was mostly thistledown, the fluff from dandelions that had gone to seed along the rim of the Pudding Basin, and any feathers or eider-down that might be floating about. As yet there was no red velvet, but the Florabellas did not worry.

"Moths and mice always see to it for us," said Mrs. Florabella, confidently. "And always the best quality."

Randy and the other girls collected flying power, too, for the ropes that would support the riding boxes: fringes, ribbons for winged bows, paper for pleated fans, bits of cloth for flags and banners. Michael and the boys of Shanty Town made paper kites for added flying power on the wheel above the center pole. They also helped Mr. O'Rafferty with the riding boxes, fashioning them out of packing cases and crates, sawing them into the right size and making them doubly strong with more boards. They even made rope handle bars for the small children.

Just as Mrs. Florabella had promised, the red velvet arrived in good time, delivered by Mr. Scroggins. There was also a long strip of red carpet. Mice and moths had been busy nibbling, making a feast of red velvet and carpets in the Town Hall, just as they had once done in a certain Royal Box at the opera.

"I knew we could rely on them," said Mrs. Florabella, and she took out her scissors from the sewing basket.

The only problem seemed to be that of the animals themselves. Until now they were only drawings on white paper. They must be made of something more durable if they were to survive wind and rain and sun and their own tremendous flying power.

"We always use wood," said Mr. Florabella. "Nice smooth wood that takes kindly to paint and brushes."

Mr. Scroggins suggested that the Florabellas have a brief pow-wow in the wigwam. It was as secret and invisible as the meeting behind the twelve closed doors of Mr. O'Rafferty's house, but this time Michael and Randy were invited. What they spoke of no one else knew, for Michael and Randy knew how to keep a secret.

Very strangely, the next morning there was a kind of leaning tower on the rim of the Pudding Basin. It was a stack of plywood —smooth, strong sheets, though not much thicker than heavy cardboard. Everyone was amazed, especially Mr. O'Hara the policeman.

"First it was the mice and moths with the velvet," he said. "And now you'll be telling me the woodpeckers have been busy sawing this lumber."

Mr. Florabella winked at Mr. Scroggins and laughed. "Someone has left his card here, and quite oddly the name is Mr. Wood. He owns a lumber mill. He says that when we finish tracing the designs of the animals on the plywood he will be happy to cut out the figures for us with a special saw."

"That will be much quicker than the soup ladle," said Mrs. Florabella.

This was not the only surprise. Behind the tower of plywood there were any number of paint brushes and buckets of rainbow-colored paint.

"Now who would be sending all this?" said Mr. O'Hara.

"There's another card," said Mr. Florabella. "It seems to be from a cousin of this Mr. Wood, a Mr. Brushwood, who owns a paint shop."

"Now isn't that odd!" said little Larry Lee. "Shouldn't his name be Mr. Paintbrush?"

The Florabellas took all the drawings of birds and animals and fish from the satchel and set them around the rim of the Pudding

82

Basin so that the children might look at them. They were to choose the twelve they liked the most. With all the Florabellas' talk of wind and wings, of fins and feathers, flying manes and waving tails, the paper drawings nearly flew away. They had to be anchored with stones and bricks.

It was not an easy choice. Three votes were taken before a final decision. Mr. Florabella's little pack of cards was used on which to write the names. Some children were too young to write anything at all except scribbles, so Mrs. Florabella wrote their choices for them. It must be said that Mrs. Florabella could not write very well herself. She could only make letters in block print, and she misspelled a shocking number of words. For instance "Camel" with a "K" instead of a "C," and "Ella-fan" for "Elephant." But no matter, the meaning was clear. The twelve winners were Camel, Elephant, Giraffe, Pony, Fawn, Rabbit, Squirrel, Swan, Dolphin, Butterfly, Wild Goose, and Ostrich.

Everyone was delighted, especially the Florabellas.

"You have made an admirable choice," Mr. Florabella announced. "We have never set up a Flying-Go-Round with greater flying power. With all these wings and feathers, flying manes and waving tails, winged hoofs and flashing fins, you will fly as no one has ever flown before. Why, I can hardly keep my feet on the ground this minute, just thinking about it."

And to prove himself right Mr. Florabella, amidst loud applause, not only turned three cartwheels on the rim of the Pudding Basin but stood on his head, bowler hat and all, the little woodcock feather fluttering in the breeze.

The Wonderful Flying-Go-Round

At last the day arrived—the day for the flight of the Wonderful Flying-Go-Round.

Every child in Shanty Town awakened early, for there was surprise and expectancy in the air. Michael and Randy O'Rafferty were the first, almost before the sun itself. They went hurrying off to Mira-Rami, each with a sugared bun, their breakfast, just as they had done that morning when they had launched the red kite and lost it—the day the Florabellas had landed in the balloon basket. That was little more than a week ago, and yet how much had happened!

This, too, was a morning of bright sunshine, the sky a clear, transparent blue with a little wind chasing a flock of fleecy, small white clouds. As the children ran, they saw in the distance their special country, greener than it had ever been before, quite as though they were seeing it again through the eye of the bamboo spying-glass. The elderberry bushes along the rim of the Pudding Basin were in bloom, the white blossoms in clusters like snowflakes. In the valley of Mira-Rami a tall tree seemed to be growing. It was the center pole of the Flying-Go-Round, with a sailcloth canopy of painted leaves.

"Look, a tree!" they exclaimed in delight.

This was the first time they had seen the canopy with its leaves and branches hiding the great wheel. Yesterday the sailcloth had been the curtain partitions of the O'Rafferty house, and now it

84

was transformed through the magic of paint and brushes. They saw the thick ropes dangling from the spokes of the wheel like the ropes of a dozen swings in the selfsame tree—only the swings were animals and birds, a dolphin and a butterfly. How beautiful they were in their bright paint, the gay saddlecloths and trappings! Red, blue, green, yellow, violet, orange, indigo—all the colors of the rainbow! How still and quiet they were, suspended in the air, and yet impatient in their waiting! Already the wind was ruffling wings and feathers, manes and tails, and waving the flags and banners, the fans and fringes tied to the ropes.

"I can hardly wait!" said Randy. "I want to ride them all, but most of all the swan."

"And I, the camel!" said Michael. "And afterwards the elephant, and then the giraffe."

As they came nearer, there was no sight of the painted wigwam among the weeds and elderberry bushes or of the Florabellas. For a moment joy was turned into anxiety.

"Oh, surely they haven't gone, have they?"

"No, of course we haven't gone! Good morning to you!" It was Mrs. Florabella's flute-like voice coming from beyond the grove of elderberry bushes. "What a lovely day for flying!"

And there were the Florabellas sitting on the rim of the Pudding Basin on the strip of moth-eaten red carpet Mr. Scroggins had brought them from the Town Hall. They were dressed exactly as they had been on the day of their arrival, and Carolino was perched as usual on the pink ostrich plume of Mrs. Florabella's marvelous velvet hat. Mrs. Florabella had the bamboo spying-glass in one gloved hand and her beaded bag in the other. She had probably been looking at the Flying-Go-Round in the valley of Mira-Rami. Mr. Florabella was fishing for sardine tins with his magnetized umbrella.

"Why, you're fishing!" Michael exclaimed in surprise. It seemed a strange thing to be doing on such an exciting day.

"So I am," said Mr. Florabella, smiling lazily. "We've been so busy lately, I haven't had a moment for fishing until today. And to a good purpose. Look!" He pointed his umbrella at the Flying-

Go-Round. Nestled comfortably on the red velvet upholstery of the riding boxes were all the cats of Mira-Rami, Taffy himself having chosen the wild white swan. "I must lure them away with sardines again. We're fond of cats, but we can't permit them to have the first ride on the Flying-Go-Round, can we?"

"Oh, no!" said the children, laughing. And then they asked hopefully, "Who *is* going to have the first ride on the Wonderful Flying-Go-Round?"

"Oh, so you think it is wonderful?" asked Mr. Florabella with sly merriment. He did not choose to answer their question.

"More wonderful than we ever expected!"

"Then you won't be interested in seeing it through the spying-glass?" said Mrs. Florabella with the same sly merriment. Without waiting for an answer, she handed the bamboo rod to them.

"How very strange!" said Randy, looking through the spying-glass. "The Flying-Go-Round isn't any different seen through the glass than it is without it! Either way, it's just as wonderful—"

"Yes, you're right," said Michael, when he in turn looked through the bamboo rod. "It's the same, with or without the glass."

The Florabellas smiled, well pleased. "That is because the dream has come true. That's one of the charms of our spying-glass."

"Mira-Rami is beginning to look almost the way it did the day we first saw it through your spying-glass," said Randy. "Lovely green, and with the rainbow down in the center ready to begin whirling—"

"Where is the wigwam?" Michael said rather anxiously. He was looking with the spying-glass through the leaves and white blossoms of the elderberry bushes. "It's completely invisible."

"We took it down this morning," said Mr. Florabella. "The balloon needs airing."

"You're not going away?"

"Well, yes, but all in good time," Mr. Florabella said. "There are other Flying-Go-Rounds to be set up, here and there and everywhere. Mostly *everywhere*."

"And other children—" said Mrs. Florabella. "Listen!"

86

It sounded like a swarm of bees that knew how to laugh and shout as well as buzz. It was the children of Shanty Town, coming to see the Wonderful Flying-Go-Round.

"And here come the cats, and just in time!" said Mr. Florabella, making drum music with the sardine tins and his umbrella. "Fish for breakfast! Lovely fish!"

Joy often has a very large sound. It did that morning at Mira-Rami. The voices of children shouting and singing, the sound carried by the wind—which had a voice of its own—filled with the rustling of paper kites and fans, the flapping of flags and banners. Not to mention the cats, who were all excitedly crying out: *MiiiRaaa-RaaaMiii!* Within a few moments after the arrival of the children Mr. O'Hara was there, all the buttons of his uniform shining, and soon the grownups of Shanty Town were there as well. All of them. They had started out the same time as the children, but they were not as fast on their feet. Nevertheless they arrived quite breathless, as though they, too, had been running.

"Glory be!" said Mrs. O'Toole. "Was there ever a prettier sight! All those lovely creatures ready to fly!"

"An elephant, mind you!" said Mr. Kelly. "Who would ever think to see one fly through the air! And that long-necked spotted giraffe as well!"

"To think that a mainmast could sprout overnight with leaves and branches!" said Mr. O'Rafferty. "I've had that old sailcloth hanging in the house for years and there was never a sight of a green bud on it, come spring or summer!"

Excited though everyone was, no one ventured from the rim of the Pudding Basin. They stood there as on a magic circle in wide-eyed delight and astonishment. Though they had all helped in some way to make the Flying-Go-Round, they could not quite believe their eyes when they saw it now, finished, ready for flight. As they stood there, exclaiming and "oh-ing" and "ah-ing," they all asked the same question. It started as a whisper: *Who is going to have the first ride?* It was the question Michael and Randy had asked the Florabellas and to which there had been no answer. The whisper was growing larger, mixed up with the sound of the wind and the fluttering wings and feathers down in the valley of Mira-Rami. *Who is going to have the first ride?*

"You'll find your answer in the bird cage," said Mr. Florabella gaily, and he held aloft the little gilded cage.

There was nothing in it.

"Everyone must write his name on a card," continued Mr. Florabella. "The card goes into the bird cage."

"Yes," said Mrs. Florabella, smiling and nodding at all the surprised faces. "The cards go into the bird cage, and Carolino knows exactly what to do with them, don't you, my pet?" Already she was handing out the little white cards that Mr. Florabella always carried in his pocket.

"I expect it's some kind of a bird act," said Mr. O'Hara, winking.

And that is exactly what it was. When all the cards were placed inside the cage, Carolino flew down from the pink ostrich plume and alighted on the top of the cage. Then, at a signal from Mrs. Florabella, the canary hopped in and out of the open door of the cage, carrying in its beak one at a time twelve cards—the names of the twelve winners who were to have the first ride. Whether Carolino knew how to read was never entirely certain, but no one seemed to mind that Michael and Randy O'Rafferty were among the first to be chosen. In truth loud cheers arose, a wave of sound that nearly lifted them from their feet. Randy would ride the wild white swan; and Michael, the camel—which was just as they had hoped.

Twelve happy children stood on the strip of red carpet, with Mr. O'Rafferty and Mr. O'Hara ready to lift the smallest into the riding boxes down in Mira-Rami. There were a dozen or more children waiting their turn, too, when Carolino would draw their names from the cage for a second flight. Expectation made everyone suddenly very still and quiet, and in that moment there was a fluttering of wings and a clear note of music. It was Carolino, perched on the top of the canopy of painted leaves, a small golden bird in a tree. Listening, they heard a little tune, trilled and warbled so merrily that everyone began humming it and putting words to it, for it was a melody that went easily with words:

> Take your feet off the ground
> On a Flying-Go-Round!
> Dreams all come true
> High in the blue
> When you—
> Take your feet off the ground
> On a Flying-Go-Round—

It was a tune that had no ending, unless you yourself put a stop to it. Both words and melody went around and around in a circle. And yet, just as Mr. O'Rafferty was about to lift the smallest child into the Butterfly riding box, the music stopped. A lovely golden note seemed to be choked in Carolino's throat. And there, coming around the rim of the Pudding Basin, was His Honor the Mayor and the twelve councilmen, chief among them Mr. Scroggins. They were all carrying small red paper kites, holding them aloft by short strings. They looked rather comical, like grownups playing a children's game. Mr. Scroggins alone was smiling. The others looked red-faced and astonished, especially the Mayor. His eyes were fairly popping out of his head.

"What have we here?" said the Mayor, but not in the loud voice that was expected of him. "What's all this?"

"It's the Wonderful Flying-Go-Round," everyone shouted, though it must be said they were all very surprised and rather anxious.

It was only the Florabellas who did not seem worried. Smiling, they walked up the strip of red carpet to greet the Mayor and the councilmen.

"How nice of you to come. You received our invitations, it seems."

For once the Mayor did not know exactly what to say. He waved the little paper kite in his hand, and finally managed to stammer, "Yes, if you call *this* an invitation! It's the first time I ever got one written on a red paper kite."

"But that's how we thought you always sent your invitations in this part of the world," said Mr. Florabella. "That's how ours arrived. If you'll excuse me a moment, I'll fetch it." He disappeared in the grove of elderberry bushes where the balloon basket was still hidden, and then returned almost at once with a large red paper kite spangled with gold and silver stars. "Here it is. It reached us while we were on a balloon flight. Whenever we see a kite made out of Christmas wrapping paper or such-like, we always know it is an invitation. Some little boy or girl has been thinking of sky flight. Dreams and wishes, you know."

"My kite!" said Michael in excitement. "It's come back!"

"Yes, of course it's yours," said Mr. Florabella. "We told you the first day we landed that we had received your invitation, don't you remember?"

"Yes, but we didn't know what you meant. How lucky that I lost it!"

90

"We're full of little surprises," said Mr. Florabella.

"That's what I was about to say," said the Mayor, stammering and stuttering.

"Which reminds me," said Mr. Scroggins, interrupting, "there's a small surprise for Miss Miranda O'Rafferty—*Randy*." He held in his hand a golden object on a slender chain. It was a little heart with a small red jewel in the center, and no one needed a spying-glass to see that it was a ruby. It was so much like Mrs. Florabella's that everyone looked at Mrs. Florabella. But there, around her neck, was her own precious locket.

"For me?" said Randy in surprise.

"Yes," said Mr. Scroggins. "It's a gift from the twelve council-men to a little girl who gave up her entire treasure so that the Flying-Go-Round might become possible. Jewels that bought plywood and paint and brushes. A little girl who had the courage to dream—"

"I think that *I* as the Mayor ought to make the presentation," stammered the Mayor.

"But it has already been presented, Your Honor," said Mr. Scroggins with twinkling eyes as he fastened the locket around Randy's neck.

"I can't quite believe it! And thank you very much," she said. "After all, I found the jewels in Mira-Rami—I mean *here*. In a way they belonged to the Flying-Go-Round."

Everyone cheered and applauded except the Mayor.

"No one is listening to me," he cried. "Who said you could go ahead with all this? I mean, you can't do it!"

"But it's already *done,* finished, ready," said Mr. Florabella, smiling. "Look!" He pointed his umbrella at the object of all attention. "There it is, the Wonderful Flying-Go-Round! That's why you've been invited."

"And quite within the law, Your Honor," said Mr. Scroggins. "You said the Dump Yard must stay where it is, and there it is! All those lovely hills and mountains of rubbish, everything in its place. Even the center pole of the Flying-Go-Round was always there, or the makings of it—fence-posts, logs, pieces of iron pipe.

Look well to it, Your Honor. It's the only part of the Flying-Go-Round that touches the ground. All the animals, the riding boxes, and the ropes are located in sky property, in the air, so to speak. And that belongs to children as much as anyone else. So there you are!"

"Do have a closer look, Your Honor," said Mr. Florabella, handing the Mayor the bamboo spying-glass.

Now quite as red as the strip of carpet on which he stood, the Mayor lifted the bamboo rod to his right eye. "Why there's nothing there but the Dump Yard, a heap of rubbish!" he exclaimed. "That's no place for children to play! I won't permit it, not even if they've got their feet off the ground!"

"Then do something about it," said Mr. Florabella cheerfully. "Make it green. That's the way these children see it now in imagination. They are *pretending,* don't you see? But if you were to haul a few loads of gravel and nice rich earth to cover all the rubbish, and sprinkle grass seed and wild-flower seeds as Mr. O'Rafferty suggested at the Town Hall—"

"That's right," said Mr. O'Rafferty. "You'd only be putting it back in its proper shape, the way it was when it was known as Dingle Dell."

"There won't be any more rags and tatters and bits of paper for you to collect," said the Mayor, his voice rather faint. "I don't suppose you've given *that* a thought, have you, Mr. O'Rafferty?"

"No, I haven't," said Mr. O'Rafferty. "All the same, I'll be busy enough with the Flying-Go-Round here, lifting the children off and on these flying creatures, and keeping the grass and flowers tidy. Besides you'll be making another Dump Yard somewhere farther out of the town. It's all within reason."

"It seems everyone has an answer to everything," said the Mayor. "I still say it won't work. . . ." His voice trailed off like a thin wisp of smoke. "It won't work. . . ."

But already the painted animals were stamping and pawing the air with impatient hoofs and feet, ready for flight. The wind was moving among the paper kites and fans, the ribbons and banners and flags on the ropes beneath the canopy; rustling, too,

among the painted leaves, blowing upon wings and feathers, the flying manes and tails, the flashing fins. The children were in the riding boxes now, or rather, it should be saïd, astride a wild white swan, a galloping camel, a winged horse, a flying squirrel, a leaping deer. Now the great wheel overhead began to turn, around and around as the earth turns and the revolving stars and the planets. *We're off! We're off!* Slowly at first, and then faster and faster, until a rainbow whirled in a perpetual circle.

> Take your feet off the ground
> On a Flying-Go-Round!

"It won't work," said the Mayor very faintly, watching in amazement the whirling rainbow. And then he, too, was trying to sing with everyone else.

> Dreams all come true
> High in the blue
> When you—
> Take your feet off the ground . . .

"Well then, *take them off the ground!*" shouted Mr. Scroggins.

"I'm trying to," said the Mayor, lifting first one foot and then the other, in a kind of hop-skip-and-jump.

"No, not like that," said Mr. Scroggins. "Dream a little! Stand on your head like Mr. Florabella."

94

And there was Mr. Florabella turning cartwheels along the rim of the Pudding Basin, looking himself like a whirling rainbow, and then disappearing in the grove of elderberry bushes.

> Take your feet off the ground
> On a Flying-Go-Round!

Faster and faster went the Flying-Go-Round, tracing its magic circle in the air, so that there was no doubt in the mind of anyone that the children were now sky riding, sky flying, probably bumping into soft little clouds and seeing wonderful sights. Everyone was watching that whirling rainbow in the valley of Mira-Rami, looking at nothing else. But suddenly Mr. O'Rafferty shouted out, "Ship ahoy!" He was pointing toward the sky where a balloon basket and a red balloon were rising upward. The Florabellas were leaning over the rim of the basket, smiling. Mrs. Florabella was waving her little pink lace handkerchief, and Mr. Florabella was waving the red-and-white checkered picnic cloth.

"Happy landings!" Everyone was shouting and waving. "Happy landings!"

There was a sudden flash of golden wings. Carolino, still singing, had left his perch atop the green canopy and was flying skyward toward the balloon basket to alight, no doubt, upon a pink ostrich plume on Mrs. Florabella's marvelous velvet hat.

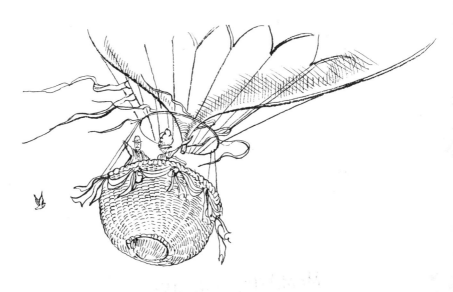

ABOUT THE AUTHOR

DANA FARALLA was born in Minnesota of Danish, French, and German ancestry. She has traveled widely, and has been at various times an actress, editor of a poetry magazine, publicity writer for an art gallery, general factotum in a rare-book shop, screen-story analyst, and a scenario writer. With many adult novels as well as several children's books to her credit, she now devotes her full time to writing.

ABOUT THE ILLUSTRATOR

HAROLD BERSON's art training in Paris started him on his career as a children's book illustrator. Born and raised in California, he has traveled in many countries and now lives with his wife in New York City.

1 2 3 4 5 69 68 67 66 65